Crosses

&

Silver Bullets

a love story ©

Franklin Webb

crossessilverbullets@gmail.com

Illustrations by Jesse Martel

jessemartelart@gmail.com

2

To everyone who believed in this little story and in the grateful guy who wrote it.

Thank-you.

Crosses and Silver Bullets

(A Love Story) ©

Act 1

Hey you.

Yeah...you.

Come closer.

Listen up.

This is a story for anyone who loves those fairy tale romances. You know...a handsome hero, a beautiful maiden, magical creatures, and a mighty battle to overcome all for that most precious of things...Love.

So, to quote a phrase made famous by two siblings...the Brothers Grimm.

Once upon a time...in a land far away. There was a mighty city where all the monsters dwelled called...Denver, Colorado.

I know. I know. What self-respecting monster would go to Denver to live? Well, if you were asked to name any ten cities that you thought monsters lived would Denver really be on the list?

That's why they live in Denver and of course...Fresno.

But we're getting off track here, let's meet our beautiful maiden. They call her Rail...because she likes to stand by the tracks and feel the vibrations as the locomotives go by. Fair warning, though, don't call her by her real name because more than likely she'll kick the crap out of you.

The word beautiful was not a lie. Those diamond blue eyes were filled with a determination and thrill for life and how can you not fall for a girl who wears combat boots so well. Her three lips piercing were just the first out of many. Nose, ears, and a few other places you're probably too young to know about. Not to be out done, of course, her tattoos were a wide assortment of designs in a variety of locations. From the black widow spider on her leg to the cartoon figure of 'Marvin the Martian' on her shoulder. She ran her fingers through her short black hair and watched in the mirror as it fell back into place clearly showing those two of highlighted streak of red and purple. With a black and gray beanie on she grabbed her coat and hit her fist into her hand saying, 'It's the night. Let's do it.'

Little did she know how true that was going out the door to meet the rest of the pack of 'Breakers'.

The Breakers were a part of a larger group called 'Howlers'. Trust me that name will make sense later. It was getting close to 1:00 in the AM at the park where the Breakers were waiting for the other part of the night's event. They hanged about jazzed for what was coming. Smoking, drinking, and playing Grunge Rock as loud they could without bringing the cops.

The cops? They really didn't need to be around tonight... it would have just complicated things.

Rail was talking to her best friend, Blond Sal, who had that wavy/curly mane that went pass her shoulders and shined of natural blond. It was the kind of hair the models, old women, and every high school girl paid a salon $150 bucks a week to have.

$500 in Beverly Hills.

"It's getting late... maybe they're not coming" Sal hopefully said.

"What... 'fraid someone will rip out a curl?" Rail joked slightly tugging at Sal's hair.

They'll show" Kyle said to them. "They got too much pride not to. Stupid tones. But don't worry if something goes wrong stick by me. I'll take care of you."

"Sure thing." said Rail then immediately shaking her head to Sal in saying, 'Yeah right.'

With a wink and a smile Kyle went off to the other Breakers. More brawn and ego than brains Kyle constantly tried to win the favor of Rail.

He loses. A lot.

"He soo wants you." said Sal.

"He's an asshole."

"Yeah." she acknowledged. "Still wants you, though."

The sound of the hard rock music suddenly became overcome by the sounds of several motorcycles. Their headlights came speeding over the hill focusing on the Breakers. The riders got off their bikes and formed a line so they could face all the Breakers.

"You can make it easier on yourselves and just leave." their leader said. "This is Brood ground now."

"Hell, it is!" Kyle yelled. "Ain't about to turn over prime land to a bunch of tones."

The Brood didn't like the word echoing through their ears.

"Well then we'll be really nice." said the Brood leader. " When we're done kicking your asses, we'll make sure you get to a good vet, fleabag!"

"Bring it." Kyle said.

Each watch the other as the Brood fangs grew out and their eyes turned bloodshot. The Breakers' fur grew out from their bodies so thick that any tattoo disappeared. Their hands turned into sharp claws while their heads changed into the shape of wolves and within seconds the two groups piled into each other.

Hitting.

Biting.

Shredding!

Each determined to win the park for their hunting ground and each completely unaware that they were the ones being hunted that night.

They're called Quinns. Short for the Inquisition. Hate to tell all of you who still practice the Wiccan ways but the Inquisition never went away it just went underground. Funded by the church it has a new charter...Destroy anything supernatural.

With **Extreme Prejudice**.

"Looks like our information was right, Father Michaels". One said. "Brood and Howlers."

"Are we ready?" Michaels asked, looking back at the squad of men readying themselves with high-powered crossbows and guns loaded with silver bullets.

"All of us." he was answered.

"Prepare yourselves." said Michaels

The Quinns kneeled, motioned crosses across their chest, and began to pray.

"We pray to the Lord for the strength and the courage to survive this night. And if we do not... may we be welcome in his loving embrace. Amen." They asked.

The Brood and the Breakers were still entrenched in their gang-fight, (neither one gaining the upper-hand) until the sky lit up with a flare. They looked up in confusion. One of the Brood was about to say 'What the fu..?' but was cut off by the arrow ripping through his heart. The others watched as his body fell to the ground and disintegrated into dust. In a heartbeat the area was filled with arrows and gunfire that was suppressed by silencers.

Like I said... no wanted the cops around.

The Brood and the Howlers quickly got over their shook as they saw the Quinns charging towards them. It was a toss-up to run or fight but the question became moot when a second squad of Quinns came from the other side. It was 'fight or die' now. Both the Brood and the Howlers knew it. So...they fought for their lives.

The fight wasn't going well. Though the vampires and the werewolves were stronger and faster, the Quinns outnumbered them and had weapons to take out a target from a distance.

One of them being Rail.

She screamed in pain as she felt the burning metal sear through her skin. She fell to the ground reverting back to her human form. She grabbed her side and rolled over seeing that the Quinns were winning. Some of the Brood and the Breakers when they saw an opening ran in a chance to escape with Quinns in close pursuit.

Rail looked around for any sign of help and amazingly saw Kyle. She reached out to him. Kyle saw her, took a couple of steps forward, but a gunshot too close for comfort spooked him and he ran right pass her disappearing in the park woods.

Before Rail could say, 'sonavabitch', someone grabbed her arm and carried her away into those same woods. With one good sniff Rail knew it was Blond Sal who saved her but something was wrong. She also knew that Sal could move a whole lot faster than this. She was limping and when she tripped and fell Rail saw why. There was an arrow through her friend's leg. Still in her werewolf mode Sal saw Rail's wound and tried to help.

"Oh Goddess, Rail, look at you" she said. "I'm so sorry. Goddess, there so much blood!"

Suddenly they heard the moving brush and footsteps heading towards them. Sal turned instantly to make a stand to the Quinns. What else would a friend do? Rail knew this and as Sal's friend knew what she had to do.

"Get outta here." she said.

"What?"

"Go."

"No!" Sal yelled.

"You can still make it but not with an arrow in you and carrying me." said Rail. "Go...Now!!"

Sal stared in disbelief.

"GO!" Rail yelled, knowing that will bring the Quinns and maybe give Sal a chance to get away.

"Over here!" they heard a Quinn yell.

They say werewolves can't cry because their wolf form doesn't have tear ducts.

What do they know?

There were tears in Sal eyes looking at her friend with pain and guilt. Even more as she ran off leaving Rail behind for the Quinns.

Three Quinns came out of the brush. The one in front told the others to track Sal while he finished off Rail. He pointed his gun at her to get a clean shot and stared for a moment.

'Do it and get it over with' she thought.

She closed her eyes and waited for the bullet to enter her body. Suddenly her eyes opened to the immense pain rushing through her body from the Quinn stepping on her wound. She looked up and saw a malice smile on his face.

With each push of his boot the Quinn enjoyed making Rail howl in agony. There's an old saying... can't really remember who said it but it goes, 'In the darkest hour... a light will appear to save you.' I've seen it happen. Rail hasn't and so never put much stock in such things like a white knight coming to save the day. That stuff only happens in fairy tales... right?

The Quinn's body fell to the ground with his chest hitting the dirt and his head twisted around facing the dark sky above. Remember that movie where that girl's head turned completely around on her body. Well...humans can't do that. So, don't try. The eyes of the dead Quinn reflected a figure over him. Rail's white knight who happened to be black.

Our hero...Danion.

Standing a good six-feet tall and sporting a leather jacket with the classic leading man features. He could hear the other Quinns returning. He knew he could probably take them but why bother. Best to leave and let things go as they may. He looked down at Rail who passed out from pain and loss of blood. Danion knew she was still alive but that wasn't going to last long.

If you asked him 'why he did it?' he probably still couldn't give you an exact answer but he did do it. He picked her up, held her in his arms, and flew off to the night sky.

Well...yeah. What else was going to happen... the end of the story? Oh... and before you start pointing it out. If vampires could fly why didn't the Brood fly off when the Quinns showed up? Well there are different types of vampires. Some can fly, some cannot, others can...We'll get into that later. Right now the best part is coming.

Me.

And how I got involved in this little tale.

"Sage, open up!" He yelled, kicking at my door.

"Who is it?"

"Danion."

I open the door and needless to say I was shocked by what I saw.

"She's been shot." he said, rushing pass me.

"Really." I said, seeing the obvious. "Come on... let's see what we can do."

I hit the wall to open up the hidden lab of my work. You see I'm a Techno-Alchemist. It's a bold new world and my place was filled with the old and the new. From classic powders to the latest high-speed Internet computer. Information and the stuff to use it with comes in handy when you have a sideline of patching up certain 'people' who can't go to a normal doctor.

"Put her on the table." I said.

He laid her down while I get a closer look at her.

"Werewolf?"

"Really?" Danion said, knowing the obvious, "Can you help her?"

"We'll see." I said, taking a look at her bloody wound. "Aww, that's...not good."

Suddenly Rail started suffocating.

"She can't breathe. Hold her still." I said.

I grabbed an oxygen mask and put it over her face. It took a few seconds but she started breathing more easily.

"Okay, that's better." I said, double checking things.

I went to the drawer and pulled out the tools you see on those hospital shows with some O-negative blood from the fridge.

"Alright... you out." I told him.

"Why?"

"'Cause... there gonna be a lot of blood here and I don't want you tempted. She needs a professional here."

"Professional what?"

"An attempt at humor." I smiled. "Ha-ha. You-Go-Now."

While Danion left I looked at Rail with some serious concern.

"I don't know if you can hear me." I told her. "But I'm gonna do my best to help ya. So... pray a lot."

Quick lesson if you ever get into this situation. The legends are true. Silver does kill werewolves. It's poison to them. It shuts down their respiratory system and reaps havoc with their hyper healing. Getting shot is bad enough but put a bullet in the heart... flat-out-dead. One will do the trick just fine but the human overkill history says, 'Three'.

I don't know how long it took me with Rail but when I saw Danion again I was hot, sweaty, tired, and really wanted a root beer.

"Well?" he asked.

"I got the bullet out and gave her something to help purge the silver from her system. If she survives the next 18 hours we won't have to worry about anything internal 'cause her hyper-healing would've kicked in. What happened here, kid?" I asked him.

Danion told me he was flying over the city when he saw a flare over the park. By the time he got there to feed his curiosity the Quinns were taking out Brood and Howlers left and right.

"Quinns?" I said. "You didn't say anything about Quinns. Do they know who you are? Did they follow you here?"

Obviously, I wasn't happy that the Quinns were involve. Their policy on people who collaborate with the 'monsters' is about the same as dealing with 'monsters' themselves but Danion promised me that everything was okay.

"I hope so, kid. I need the Quinns on my ass as much as the Consortia or 109." I said.

"I know… but that Quinn didn't just want to kill her. He wanted her to suffer as much pain as possible first." Said Danion.

"Nearly two-hundred years on this earth and you're just realizing that man's inhumanity to man doubles when they don't consider something 'human'."

Danion acknowledged that.

"So… any other reason you saved her?" I asked.

"As in?"

"As in she's very attractive."

"So?"

"So, she's… very attractive. In a 'I can rip your throat out' sort of way."

"She's a werewolf." said Danion.

"So?"

"I'm a vampire."

"And…?"

"And never shall the two meet." said Danion

"Says who?"

"Anyone who wants to keep their brain inside their head." he said, stressing that I should stop this conversation.

"Okay, I get it." I said. "So... you think she has a boyfriend?"

After giving me that 'Don't be an idiot' expression I decided to let it go...for now.

"So... want to see her?" I asked.

Danion nodded and when we saw Rail her eyes were slightly open and aware.

"She's semi-conscious... that's good." I said. "Here... hold her hand."

"W-Why?" he asked.

"To show her she's not alone in her wish for a speedy recovery." I said. "Geez, it's not like a first date."

Yet.

I left them alone so I could clean and put away those doctor tools. I looked back and saw that Danion was easing well into the empathy roll with Rail.

They say a woman knows instantly when a guy is 'The One'. When Rail looked up at Danion and realized he was a vampire she immediately used all her strength to put three clawed gashes into his faces to make him let go of her hand.

Okay... sometimes it takes a little bit longer.

2

It was rounding out to be six in the PM and I was just finishing off my gourmet meal of mac-n-cheese when I felt someone behind me. I turned around and was welcomed by a shaped claw around my throat pinning me off my feet and against the wall.

"So... you're up and about." I said to Rail.

I quickly noticed the yellow eyes and fanged teeth features on her human face. Also, that I really need to get some of those hospital robes for people whose clothes I cut away. A gleam of her nakedness with the thought of her ripping out my throat gave me a feeling of both terror and excitement.

Not the first time that's happen.

"Who are you? How did I get here?" she demanded.

"Sage. A friend of mine. In that order."

"The vampire." she said, sniffing the air.

"That's right."

"Not Brood."

"No... he's House."

She wanted to know where he was and I told her that he left before the sun came up. Besides, after that little love-tap she gave Danion he didn't really want to be stuck in a room with her all day.

"Listen." I said. "If your gonna continue your interrogation in this fashion at least change arms. The one you're using is putting stress on those sutures.

"I don't think so." she said.

I could feel her arm getting tired and see the slight stress of pain in her face that she was trying to hide. So, I had to insist on the issue by putting the gun to her chest.

"Now you've been shot once already and I really doubt you want to go through the experience again. And... I'm aiming at the right spot. At least I hope I am 'cause it's taking all my willpower not to look down pass your neck." I said.

Rail put me down and slowly backed away. I could tell she wanted to rip me to shreds but we both knew that wasn't going to happen with the gun on her and the way she was favoring her side.

"Alright. First, there are some shirts in the closet." I said. "Put one on, please."

I learned a long time ago to respect women. Respect them or they'll kill you in your sleep. So, seeing Rail in the *all together* wasn't a good thing.

Of course, I wasn't really believing that at the time.

She didn't trust me enough to turn her back on me, so I had to get her to trust me by putting the gun down and slowly turning my back to her.

"I'm not your enemy." I said, hoping she wouldn't jump me and rip me to shreds.

A couple of minutes passed with no claws in my back and my shorts still clean.

"Alright, you can turn around." she said.

With that I turned and saw that she was wearing one of my favorite shirts but decided not to push the matter while we both looked at each other and the gun.

"So... what now?" she asked.

"Now obviously you're feeling better." I said, rubbing my neck. "Your clothes... minus one shirt and more than some blood have been cleaned and pressed. You can go on your merry little way."

She got dressed, tied up her boots, and headed for the front door, but I knew there was something lingering on her mind.

"So, that's it?" I asked.

"What? You wanna 'Thank-you'? Thank-you. Happy?"

"You're welcome", feeling her hollow 'Thank-you'. "But what I was referring to is why you think a vampire saved you last night?"

"Doesn't matter."

"Doesn't it?"

"Fine... why?"

"Cause you're cute."

She looked at me stunned.

"At least... I think that's the reason." I said. "If you wanna know his you're gotta have to ask him."

"Well, I'll be sure to do that next time I see him." she said, opening the door to leave.

"Hey."

As she stopped I went to the fridge, pulled out a water bottle, and tossed it to her.

"It's raw ground chuck mixed in a blender with orange juice." I said. "The protein and Vitamin C will speed up your recovery."

She looked at the bottle, headed out the door, and then stopped.

"Thank-you." she said sincerely and left.

"You're welcome."

I felt sad seeing her leave (especially with my shirt) and happy that she didn't call my bluff on my very 'empty' gun. Tends to work better when the gears and things aren't removed. It echoed through my mind when she said 'The next time I see him.' believing full well that she probably never to see Danion again.

Oh, come on.... really?

The Breaker hangout which was once filled with life and hard rock music was now a place of mourning. Thanks to the Quinns their ranks had been cut to less-than half. Sal was sitting in the corner rocking back and forth still crying about leaving her best friend behind. Images passed through her mind as she thought about all the good times between her and Rail. Then more tears rolled down her face from knowing that she would never see her friend again.

She wiped her face dry when she suddenly caught a whiff of something. She sniffed the air to see if it was her imagination. Sal got up and started towards the door wondering if it was just wishful thinking and praying it wasn't. She opened the door and her eyes fixed on the sight that was in front of her.

"What's wrong? You look like you've seen a ghost." Rail smiled at her.

"Goddess, I hope not." Sal said, giving Rail a huge hug. "You're alive! You're alive!"

"I won't be if you keep crushing me." she said

"I'm sorry. Are you okay?" Sal asked, checking out Rail's side.

"I'm fine. So are you?" asked Rail

Rail looked down and saw that the arrow in Sal's leg was gone and healed. The rest of the Breakers swarmed around them happy to see that someone else got away from the Quinns. Rail was happy, too... until she noticed the small number of Breakers.

"Is it just us?" she didn't want to ask.

The room was quiet.

"Mic. Jane. Copper..." one said, naming the dead.

There were others but they couldn't bring themselves to named them.

"Kyle?" Rail asked.

"We don't know." said Sal. "But if you made it maybe he did, too."

"Ohh... yeah." Rail said, remembering how he left her in the park. "He's real good at taking care of himself. *Real* good."

Rail knew that sooner or later Kyle had to stick his head out. And when that happened she was going to show him how happy she was that he was alive... by ripping his head off.

Two days have passed and the Breakers remembered the lives of their friends by partying from club to club. The latest spot was The Undergrounder for 'Lore' only.

The Lore.

It's what the super-naturals called their community. Sure they still proudly wore their individual names of vampire, werewolves, and so many others to represent themselves. But just as the different races are all called human, they are all part of the Lore.

Short for Folklore.

The standard rule in these places was neutral territory even though most of them didn't like each other. After two days Rail was completely healed and dancing up a storm next to Sal liked she never been shot.

Everyone on the dance floor was enjoying themselves when an arguing couple was gathering attention. From the expressions and rolling eyes these two were well known (and loud). They fought over the most mundane things for who knows how long until she decided to stop it by kissing her hubby on the lips.

"It's the quickest way to shut him up." she told the crowd.

With sighs and giggles the night went on as Rail and Sal headed to the bar for a couple of drinks.

"Here's to lost friends." Sal said, lifting her glass.

Rail lifted hers' in acknowledgment. They toasted and Sal quickly gulped her drink.

"Another." Sal said, slapping her hand on the bar.

"You sure?" asked Rail.

"I'm sure."

Rail knew Sal wasn't a big drinker but figured that she was covering her grief with booze. So, Rail stuck close to her to make sure Sal didn't go overboard when something (someone) caught her eye.

It was Danion.

"Stay here." Rail said to Sal.

"Why? Where are you going?"

"Not far. I just... gotta check out something."

Rail moved passed the crowd until she was able to see Danion. He was talking to a gnome in the back of the club. She couldn't make out what they were saying and before she could get a closer look Sal grabbed her by the arm to tell her the news.

"Rail, it's Kyle. It's Kyle!" she yelled.

Sal lead her back to the Breakers who were happy to see Kyle. Rail was happy, too. Especially when she laid her fist in his jaw. Landing on his back and tasting blood he couldn't recover fast enough to keep Rail from kicking his ass. With a fist, a boot, and anything at hand she turned Kyle into a bloody mess. After the getting pass their shock the Breakers grabbed Rail with the obvious question on their faces, 'Why?'.

"This sonavabitch left me out here to save his own ass!" she screamed.

She explained in detail what happened that night. The other Lore were not looking at Kyle with great sympathy.

"If it wasn't for Sal and---some real good luck I'd be dead now." Rail said, catching herself before she mentioned Danion.

"Well you're alive now. That's all that matters, right?" asked Kyle.

He was trying save face by pointing that out the crowd.

It wasn't working.

"What matters is that everyone knows what a fucking coward you are. And maybe if you get shot in the gut you'll understand how pissed-off I am!" cried Rail.

"Ok. Ok." Sal said, pulling Rail away. "You made your point. Don't know what good it did, though. He'll heal in an hour."

Realizing that Rail put one final boot between Kyle's legs causing phantom pains to go through the males of the club.

"That won't heal so fast" said Rail.

As Kyle twisted in pain Sal pulled Rail aside to talk.

"Okay... truth time." said Sal.

"About?"

"I left you behind---"

"Cause I told you to. Don't feel guilty abo---"

"No." said Sal, not wanting to remember but needing an answer. "I left you behind. Bullet in you. Gushing blood. Quinns coming. You're alive. How?" she asked.

"You wouldn't believe me." said Rail.

"Try me."

She had to tell somebody. So, Rail told Sal everything that happened after she left Rail. The look of complete amazement and shock was so deep that Sal could barely utter a word.

Quick history lesson. 500 years ago, the werewolves and the vampires were on the brink of war. Then the Inquisition came and all the Lore decided to lay low from the mortal world that was getting larger, stronger, and more organized. The werewolves and the vampire made an uneasy truce but little bouts like the park have been happening for centuries.

They hate each other.

A vampire takes great pleasure in the death of a werewolf. And a werewolf would rather chew their own arm off then help a vampire. So, the question is still out there. Why did Danion save Rail?

"I don't know." Rail said. "But I'm gonna find out."

She went back to where see saw Danion but he was gone but the gnome he was talking with was still there.

"Hey… where did the vamp go?" she asked.

"What's it to you?" the gnome asked.

"Need to talk to him."

"What's it worth?"

"Your eyes still in your head."

The gnome started laughing at her threat.

"Honey, I've had bigger scares from my ex's lawyer." he smiled. "Besides… it's not like you're gonna see him again."

"What do ya mean?" she asked, in a confused tone.

"Let's just say where he's going… I really don't put much odds of him ever coming back."

It was a building in the middle of the warehouse district. Owned by the Church under the name of its many shell companies. Not only did it house weapons for the Quinns but Quinns themselves. Redesigned like an indoor army base it had beds, gym, strategy room, and of course a chapel. Still technically a warehouse it had stacks of crates forming a small maze in the building. Security was light because no one knew where they were. Beside... the Quinns knew no 'abomination' would actually willingly go to a place where the Quinns set up shop.

They were wrong.

Danion stepped out of the shadows watching the Quinns go by. He walked through the corridors of crates looking for something and yet not knowing what it was. He spotted a half-opened box, took a look inside, and quickly reeled back from the sight of dozens of crosses inside. Spooked and shaking his head in disbelief one question kept echoing through his head.

'What the hell am I doing here?'

The gashes across Danion's face were completely gone by the time he got home. He was ready for a long day's sleep when he felt someone/something in the room.

"Who's there?"

"I'm here." a voice said.

Another vampire stepped out of shadows wearing a black suit and looking like one of those older corporate execs except for more distinguished than sleazy.

"Walsh?"

"It's been some time." said Walsh.

As if seeing Walsh wasn't enough of a surprise Danion suddenly noticed a light behind Walsh. Small and bright it moved up and rested on Walsh's shoulder showing herself to be a fairie. Her long blond hair was in a ponytail that went down her back between her silk wings. Being six inches tall, she wore a black business-like suit with matching heels and had five piercings in each ear. She pulled down her tiny sunglasses slightly and sized Danion up with her Diamond-blue eyes that seemed to stare right through you.

Definitely not your 'fairy tale' fairie.

"I like you to meet my associate." said Walsh. "Zarafinn."

Danion greeted her with a head nod fully knowing this wasn't a social call.

"So... what do you want?" he asked. "More to the point what does the Consortia want?"

The Consortia.

The self-appointed protectors of the Lore with one goal. That anything supernatural stays in the ranks of fairy tales, comic books, and Hollywood. With their members being worldwide and spreading throughout the entire Lore society. They were dedicated, powerful, and more than willing to use extreme measure to protect their people.

"Last night a squad of Quinns attacked a pack of Howlers and Brood." said Walsh.

He was about to say he knew but realized they didn't need to know he was there so Danion decided to keep it that way.

"I... see." Said Danion

"The Quinns have a new Denver leader named Michaels." said Walsh. "He's smart, driven, and has a strong following in the ranks."

"Sound likes a problem." said Danion.

"Not really. We've dealt with Quinns like him before. The problem is last night's attack was number nine in a two month period." Walsh said. "They've been too precise and frequent to be either by luck or chance. Leaving only one conclusion."

"A snitch?" asked Danion.

"We like you to find this informant and 'deal with it'." said Walsh.

"'Deal with it?' Is that what the kids are calling it these days?"

A snicker came from Zarafinn.

"Do this and it will be number 2 of 3, for '91." said Walsh.

"Why me?"

"You're smart. You know Denver. You have contacts here on both sides that can help. And---"

"I'm expendable if something goes wrong." knew Danion.

"And I know when the motivation is right you won't stop until you've hunted a something or someone down and obliterated it. I think getting out from under foot of the Consortia would be that motivation." said Walsh.

"And with that we end this conversation with me saying, 'I will do it.'" said Danion.

"Good. The sun will be up soon and we better leave." Said Walsh, as he and Zarafinn headed to the window to hit the open air.

"Wait... how can I get in touch with you?" asked Danion.

"Don't worry... we can always find you." said Zarafinn.

Danion heard the threat in that statement a knew there was more to this situation than they were letting on.

He was right.

"Don't you think we should've told him all of it?" Zarafinn asked Walsh.

"If he's as smart as I know he is he'll figure it out himself."

"And then 'Deal with it?'"

"We'll see." Said Walsh. "We will see."

Danion used the first night to talk to his human and Lore contacts. He told each of them what they needed to know and they didn't ask too many questions. It was the way things were and everybody like it that way. It was the second night he got a call to meet Frank the Gnome at the Undergrounder.

"Got what I asked for?" asked Danion.

"Yeah." Frank said, handing him a piece of paper. "Do I even want to know why you want this?"

Danion gave him the look of 'No'.

"Thought so." Frank said. "When you die can I have your stuff?"

"Don't plan on dying anytime soon."

"Oh... really? Haven't you heard what's been happening out there?"

"Quinns."

"Yeah... and going to this place is like one of you guys, and I don't mean vampires, to a Klan meeting."

"You would think but that's different." said Danion. "I'm gone and Frank if I do die...you're not getting my stuff."

They both gave a half laugh to each other when they heard the commotion across the club. They couldn't see who was involve but they could hear a young woman screaming about a 'son of a bitch'.

"Wonder what's that's about?" said Frank.

He turned to Danion but he was gone like in a scene in Hollywood movie leaving Frank shaking his head.

"Vampires." he said.

Danion tired of making his way through the crate maze flew up on top of them. Too high for the Quinns to notice and easier to avoid he made his way over the crates until he found the open part of the Quinn warehouse. He looked down at them in lurker mode and spotted one that seemed to be the leader as a cellphone call that was giving that leader a big smile.

"Good, I'll tell them." he said, getting off the cell. "Good news! We've just taken out a troll pit under Tyson bridge."

The Quinns cheered for their victory as a Quinn with a clipboard wanted to talk to the squad leader.

"Sir, I've just done an inventory check." he said. "And were missing a can of cover spray."

"Yes… Father Michaels gave it to our 'friend'. Guess it didn't want the others to know it's working for the 'God Squad'. SL (squad leader) said.

"But sir, those cans---."

"I know. I know. A 1000 dollars a pop but I agree with Michaels that we can't lose this source."

"It's betrays its' own." Clipboard said. "Another reason they should be destroyed. All of them."

"Really?" Danion said, watching Clipboard walk to a safe area… for Danion.

He didn't see it coming. Danion was just there pinning Clipboard against the wall. Staring into his eyes to control his mind.

Hypnotism.

One of the powers that some vampires have but it doesn't work on everybody, like other Lore and strong-willed humans but Clipboard fell like a house of cards.

"Who's the one who's been helping you hit the Lore?" Danion asked.

"I don't know. Only Father Michaels does."

"Damn it."

Danion knew there was no way he was going to get to Michaels. He was probably surrounded by a 100 Quinns. No way to get close enough to get information but what choice did he have?

"Where is Michaels now?" he asked.

"He's probably going to---"

Before Clipboard could finish his answer two Quinns turned the corner. Danion popped his fangs and rushed them before they could be startled. They landed twenty feet away... and right in the middle of the other Quinns.

"Vamp!" one of them yelled in the direction of Danion.

Immediately they all grabbed their crossbows and high-powered soak -guns filled with holy water. Danion ran into the crate maze where he thought he could lose the Quinns by flying up a skylight. No luck there as he heard Quinns on top of the crates looking down at the pathways in hopes of getting a clear shot. He turned corner and corner until he stopped at the sight of a Quinn with a crossbow. Danion knew he could dodge the arrow and take him out before the Quinn's second heartbeat. The Quinn knew it too, that's why he pulled out an ace called the Holy Cross. Danion turned around to get away from the sight of righteousness and was faced by another Quinn with a soaker. One side, an arrow that could turned him to dust. The other, holy water that could melt him away like the Wicked Witch of the West.

You could tell neither sides were appealing.

"It's over here!" the one with the cross yelled.

The two stepped closer to put Danion in a squeeze play.

"Do you have any last words in hopes that your soul will be saved abomination?" the one with the soaker asked.

"Yes." Danion said calmly. "Tell Frank, he gets the Blu-ray and nothing else."

The Quinns obviously not knowing what he was talking about were distracted for a moment.

More than enough time for Danion's rescue.

All the Quinn felt was a claw on the side of his head with the other side being slammed against the side wall of a crate. The one with the crossbow was dead. His body slid to the ground, leaving a bloody imprint and trail behind. The crossbow now in the clawed hand fired its arrow. It flew passed Danion into the chest of the other Quinn killing him and leaving Danion in shock to his savior.

"What the hell are you doing here?" he cried.

"Saving your ass!" Rail stated the obvious.

"You got a death wish or something?"

"Look who's talking?"

Suddenly both of them heard from so far away the cocking of a gun.

"Look out!" they both cried, pushing each other out of the way of a stream of holy water.

Learning this Rail went back to face the Quinn. Before Danion could say, 'What are you doing?' she was soaked with water. The surprised Quinn looked at her wondering why she wasn't melting away. He quickly got his answer when Rail transformed into full werewolf mode.

"Real good." Danion said, in an unhappy tone. "They probably thought we were both vampires."

"Yeah... now they know arrows and holy water won't work on me." she said, feeling full of herself.

"Exactly."

"We got a wolf here!" the Quinn yelled. "We need silver... Now!"

Rail closed her eyes to her own stupidity.

"Come on!" Danion said, grabbing her arm.

They started running down the aisle. Rail in werewolf mode using all fours outran Danion and was the first to hit the open area of the warehouse. She was also the first one to face a gun barrel loaded with silver bullets. Suddenly she was pulled back by her belt as Danion stepped between her and those bullets.

Silver bullets don't kill vampires but they still sting like a bitch. He showed how much by tearing off the Quinn's arm and beating him with it. Then a pain went shooting through Danion's arm caused by a crossbow arrow. They looked and saw Quinns gathering with guns and arrows ready to kill. They ran to a single crate ducking behind it for protection only to find their side of the crate was facing a concrete wall.

"We're fucked!" yelled Rail.

"We gotta get outta here!" Danion cried. "How did you get in?"

"Air-vent but we'll never reach it. You?"

"Skylight but forget it."

"Why?"

"'Cause I can't move fast enough carrying you." he answered. "They'll just knock us out of the air."

"So... I guess I'm being left behind, right?"

"I just took several bullets for you. You really think I'm going to ditch you now to save myself?"

"Might. It's happened to me before." she said.

"Well... just 'might' happen again." he said, feeling insulted.

Danion then started screaming as his skin started melting from holy water splashing off the wall from a soaker-gun on the other side.

"That will soften the vamp." SL said. "Get those guns ready for the wolf!"

Danion and Rail used their jackets to keep the water off him all along hearing the Quinns slowly coming at both sides to rush them.

"We're dead." she said

"Not yet. I just need to concentrate."

"For what?! We---"

"Shut up!" he yelled "I-need-to-concentrate!"

Like I said before mind control is one of the better powers for some vampires but difficult to maintain if you don't have 'line of sight'... especially if you're from the House.

Difficult... but not impossible.

The Clipboard Quinn that everyone forgot about walked on the scene carrying a handgun. Danion could see through Clipboard's eyes but the grip on his mind was weakening. He knew if he told Clipboard to shoot at the other Quinns he just might be strong enough to resist leaving Danion and Rail up the creek. So, Danion decided to give him another target.

The bullet ruptured the pure oxygen tank causing an explosion that set off another and then another. The Quinns ducked for cover as crates caught on fire. Danion grabbed Rail as tight as he could and flew straight through the skylight passing go and not collecting 200 dollars.

The fire spread quickly through the warehouse since the Quinns didn't invest in sprinkler system. The blaze could be seen from the several rooftops including the one Danion and Rail landed on.

"We made it." a disbelief Rail said, turning back into her human form

"Barely." he said, in another unhappy tone. "Listen… I don't know who you are. Frankly, I really don't care. We nearly both got killed back there. How the hell did you even know where this place was?"

"Thank your gnome friend."

"I'm going to kill him."

"What were you doing there?" she asked.

"None of your business."

"Really?"

"Yeah, really!"

Arguing started to ensue between with them. Back and forth they went getting louder and louder. Him yelling. Her screaming. Him making comments. Her shouting 'UP YOURS!'. Until straight out of nowhere Rail kissed Danion right on the lips.

It wasn't a long kiss.

It wasn't a short one either.

But when she pulled away it left Danion with a stunned face of 'What the hell?'.

"Just wanted to shut you up." she said.

And with that she punched him the jaw.

"That's for the warehouse." she said. "Never tell me to shut up again."

Danion looked at her still speechless until he finally flew off into the night sky while shaking his head in disbelief.

As for Rail, she started making her way back to the Breakers when it suddenly dawned on her that she didn't find out why Danion saved her the other night. It didn't really matter in the face of surviving another Quinn encounter... but it left more questions than before.

One, why was Danion in a place crawling with Quinns?

Two, why did she follow him?

Three... and the one that was forefront in her mind. Did she just kiss a vampire?

Now she was shaking her head in disbelief telling herself she just kissed a vampire. Then slowly a girlish smile came across her lips. You know the kind I mean. She just kissed a vampire she told herself.

And it wasn't that bad.

Not that bad at all.

3

She was a twenty-something with short slightly curled dark hair. Eyes darker than a clear night's sky. The skin that was around her body was softer than silk that held a siren-like English accent.

She liked me.

And the real plus she wasn't exclusively into men.

"The world had better be ended." I stressed to Danion after saying 'Good-bye' to my first date in---Nevermind.

"I need your help." he said

"My help? My help!" I said, completely disillusion. "She's an Earth-witch who was about to show me the gratitude ceremony for Mother Nature. It's about an hour long. Done completely...in-THE-NUDE!"

"Getting the point but I still need your help. I need to know what this."

"A spray can!" I pointed out the obvious.

"But what's in it?" he asked.

I took the can and headed to my lab.

"I swear if this is a can of Right Guard..." I said.

I pulled out my Micro-Chemical-analyzer and sprayed the contents in the scanner. While waiting for the spray to be broken down and identified I was annoyed and angry that my steady supply of Elf-porn was probably going to be employed that night. Until my eyes widened to the display on the computer screen.

"What the hell is this?" I said shocked. "Half these chemicals can't be identified. What is this stuff?"

"That's what I want to know."

"Where did you get this?"

"You don't want to know." he said.

"I know there's a standing rule about asking too many questions but me being slightly paranoid, I ask again feeling I'm gonna dread the answer... where did you get this?" I asked.

Danion told me everything. The Quinns' warehouse, Rail showing up, and them barely escaping. My being shocked before paled in comparison.

"But I inadvertently put this in my pocket before all hell broke loose. Now, I really need to know what this is and what it does. They called it a... cover spray?" said Danion.

"Invisibility?" I asked myself. "Nah, not the right chemicals."

"What?"

"Nothing. When would you need this?"

"Yesterday."

I rubbed my eyes and took a deep breath.

"Then you better close the shades 'cause we could be here all night and day." I said. "Got some friends in cyberspace that could help but I gotta be careful. The Quinns red flag the net for anything that involves them. So... your little wolf-girl was with you, huh?"

"She's not my wolf-girl." he said.

"But she was there?"

"Yes."

"Wonder why?"

"Don't ask me." Danion said, shaking his head. "She's obviously insane. I mean who would follow me to a Quinn stronghold?"

"Why would one go to a Quinn stronghold in the first place?" I asked the obvious.

"Point taken. But why was she there?"

"Cause you're cute."

"What?" Danion looked perplexed.

"Nevermind." I said. "Who knows? She probably paying you back. Y'know how a lot of werewolves are into the loyalty thing. 'You did something for me, I do something for you'."

"We'll if that the case... debt paid. I don't need a loose cannon around kissing me one minute and hitting me the nex..."

Danion quickly shut up when he realized what he said but it was too late. My eyes and ears peaked and were determined to hear more.

"Kiss? What kiss. You didn't say anything about a kiss. What happened?"

"W-Why do you want to hear this?" he asked, growing ever more uncomfortable.

"'Cause I won't have a sex-life till who knows when and I need to live vicariously through someone else. You're elected. Now what happened?"

Sighing and knowing that I probably wouldn't be working very hard on the mystery spray can until I got the story (and he was right, of course) Danion started talking.

"After we got away from the Quinns we landed on a roof, started arguing, and next thing I know she's kissing me."

Danion was quiet for a moment. What he was thinking I could only guess but whatever it was it put a slight curl of a smile on his lips.

"Then she decked me" he said, snapping out of it. "Like I said... insane."

"Maybe..." I smiled. "Just maybe."

"Are you outta your mind?!" Sal yelled to Rail, hitting her over the head with a rolled up magazine.

"Stop!" Rail cried, covering her head.

"Not till I knock sense in your damn head!"

Rail told Sal about what happened with Danion and the Quinns. Her reaction was less than unpleasant.

"First you follow that vamp to the Quinns. Then you actually go inside the place. Didn't getting shot teach you anything?! Haven't they killed enough already? Do you personally need to put your name on their hit list?!" she screamed.

"Okay, I get it. I get it!" Rail said, snatching the magazine away.

Rail looked at her and saw that Sal was close to tears.

"You're really upset." she said.

"Yes!" Sal shouted.

"Alright...I'm sorry." said Rail. "I won't do anything like that stupid again."

"Yeah, right." she said, knowing full that was not going to happened.

The two of them sat down with Sal still amazed by Rail's story.

"What were you thinking?" Sal asked, wanting yet not wanting to know the answer.

"I don't know. Honestly... I was just wondering what he was doing there." said Rail.

"Well, it's a miracle either of you made it out alive."

"Yeah, flew right through the skylight to..."

It was like a moment of wonderment came over Rail. You know, when kids (regular kids) realize there's magic in the world.

"Oh my god we were flying." Rail smiled. "Sal... I was flying."

"Sound exciting."

"It was till he started yelling at me."

"About?"

"Following him."

"Good. Maybe he got some sense through that thick skull of yours." Sal hoped. "No, wait... look who I'm talking to. Hit him for yelling at you, right?"

"Hell yeah, right after I... never mind."

"What? What?"

"I... kissed him." said Rail.

"You kissed him?"

Sal looked at her quiet and stunned for a few seconds. Then she started laughing. Slowly at first then hysterically as if she heard the funniest thing if the world.

"Okay...between the Quinns, the bullets, the flying, and of course the kiss. Did you even find out the thing you wanted to know in the first place?" Sal asked.

"No." Rail said, lowering her head in embarrassment.

Tears started coming out of Sal's eyes from laughing so hard. Rail started laughing a little herself until she saw that 'son of a bitch' named Kyle."

"What the hell is he doing here?" she asked Sal.

"I know you're not happy to see him now but---"

Rail gave clear expression on that statement.

"Alright... very understatement." said Sal. "But he's one of us. Not just a Breakers... a Howler."

"I'm a Howler. You're a Howler. He-is-not-a-Howler. Remember... loyalty to the family, friends, and all through the pack."

"I know that." Sal more than understood. "But he made a mistake. It's wasn't intentional."

"Is that what he told you? So, where was Mr. 'Unintentional' for two days after he bolted?" asked Rail.

"Under a bridge with some trolls."

"A hole in the ground? Figures."

"Hey, I know forgiving him right now is hard---"

"Some things you don't forgive."

There was a clear look of conviction on her face and Sal knew at this point Rail was unmovable.

"Let's just change the subject." said Sal.

"Please."

"So... Rail and her vampire sitting by a tree. K-I-S-S-I-N-G. First comes lov---

"Shut-up." said Rail, mostly so the other Breakers weren't hear.

"Kissing a vampire." Sal whispered. "You freak."

"Shut-up."

"After all that you still didn't find out why he saved you."

"Yeah." Rail said, thinking about it.

Sal looked Rail and instantly knew what was going through her head.

"Oh, Goddess... the look." Sal said. "I know that look. Don't you even think about looking for him again. He led you to Quinns the first time, who knows how you'll end up next? Remember... not going to do anything that stupid again."

"You're right." said Rail. "Besides... I wouldn't even know where to start."

"Good." Sal said, shaking another magazine at her. "I'm hungry. You wanna get something to eat?"

"Sure."

"What do you have in the mood for?"

Rail thought about it and I think you can pretty much guess the answer.

"Ground chuck and orange juice." she said.

It was the early morning hours as the Quinns were recovering from their warehouse disaster by already setting up shop at their new site. The squad leader overseeing things was clearly distraught over recent events. Something that was not missed by Father Michaels.

"Is something wrong my son?" he asked.

"Yeah, I have fifteen men down by broken bones, being unconscious, and the ever popular... death."

"This isn't your fault... it's mine. All of our success I should've known that the abominations were going to retaliate."

"We were caught off guard last night." SL said. "Security was light and we didn't put any thought that we might be attack. We deserved this."

Michaels stared at him and then slapped him across the face.

Listen!" Michaels ordered. "We lost men. We lost supplies. We lost a base. But did we lose faith?"

"No."

"Did we lose faith?"

"No!"

"Did-We- Lose Faith?!" he yelled to all the Quinns.

"NO!" they all yelled.

"We can't and we won't ever lose faith. Because if we do...this war is over and the world will fall into darkness. We are the only line against it. The Lord sends us obstacles to test our faith but we endure because of our faith. The same faith that brought us 'our friend' to help destroy the abomination."

"Forgive me, Father." the SL said.

"I'm not the one you should be asking forgiveness from." Michaels said, tilting his head upward.

"Speaking of 'our friend'... any chance it was involve last night?"

"Doubtful. It's not that smart or that stupid. Especially with what I have to keep it in line."

"That being?"

"My secret that's need to know."

"Understood." said the SL with no hesitation. "When's your next meeting?"

"Tonight."

"And you're going alone again."

"I am."

"I don't like it. Something happens to you we lose our source."

"Then I'll endeavor to make sure nothing happens to me."
Michaels said "On another matter... how's my family?"

"Good. They were moved again last night after the warehouse
blew. They say the little one's a handful.

"That he is." Michaels said, with a chuckle. "But let's finish this
move before nightfall."

"I still don't like it." the SL said. "But I won't complain as long as
the intel stays good."

"Don't worry, my son. The 'intel' will always be good." Michaels
said. "Our Lord has guaranteed it."

When I opened the door, I half hoped it was my Earth-Witch
coming back to be nude for an hour. Imagine my surprise and
some-what disappointment to see Rail.

"What are you doing here?" I asked.

She lowered her head asking herself the same question.
Embarrassed, Rail finally answered the question shaking her head
in disbelief.

"The vampire. Where can I find him?"

Hey, kid." I called to Danion. "You ain't gonna believe this."

Rail walked in clearly surprised to see Danion in my living room.
They looked at each other quietly not knowing what to say to each
other. Me? I was off to the side waiting for the tension to break.
Until they both gave me the 'this is private' look.

"Jeez... I'll just go over there." I said, pointing to my lab. "Isn't like it's my house or anything."

"I wanna talk to you." Rail said, starting towards him.

"Stay there, please." he said. "I don't need to get hit again. Or... anything else."

"Fine... I just cut to the chase. Why did you save me the other night?"

"Does it matter?"

"Yeah, it matters." she said. "In case you haven't notice Werewolf... Vampire. We don't like each other... A lot. And we don't go out of our way to save each other either. But by my count we've done it at least six times. You, two. Me, four."

"Waitaminute... you saved my life four times? How?" he asked.

"The two Quinns." she pointed out as if it wasn't obvious.

"You're counting that as two?" he said perplexed. "That was one event. You can't count that as two."

"Pushing you outta the way from that holy water above."

"Excuse me? I pushed you out of the way."

"And don't forget me using my jacket to cover you from the splashing holy water."

"That was a save?"

"Ohh... you are so petty." She said.

"I'm so petty?" he said, completely astonished. "This from the girl who thought I was going to leave her behind to save myself after I took 1-2-3-**Four** silver bullets for her. And let's not forget my little part in flying us out of the warehouse after I got that Quinn to blow those air tanks."

Rail couldn't argue. He was right but her ego refused to let him have the last word.

"Y'know... you should really stick you head back up your ass to keep all these good deeds from leaking out." she said.

And they were off again. He yelled. She screamed. Louder and louder. I probably would have gotten between them if it wasn't for the small fact that she a werewolf and he's a vampire...duh. As they argued they starting moving closer to each other. They finally stopped fighting when they realized just how close they were to each other. Eye to eye. Fang to fang. They just stood there silently looking at each other. Who knows what could have happened if I didn't break the quiet with a victory cry.

"Eureka!! Gold at last!" I cried, with a little Elmer Fudd laugh.

Danion rushed into the lab with Rail behind him wondering what the excitement was all about.

"I know what it does and you two better sit down for the news." I told them.

"What 'what' does?" Rail asked.

Danion told her why he was there and what he wanted me to do.

"Alright." she understood (part of it). "So, what's it do?"

"And keep it under five minutes, please." said Danion.

"Hey... is it my fault I love my craft?" I said. "But I'll get to the point. Y'know how all Lore can just basically smell or sense humans. That's how they avoid them so easily when you want. To find them when you want. Or to..."

I was hesitant to finish my thought but Rail finished it for me.

"Hunt them down and rip out their livers when we want." she said.

"Yeah... that's it." I said. "But if you spray this stuff on ya, scent-wise... you're invisible."

"No way." she Rail.

"Way." I said.

"You're saying if I spray this shit on me no other Lore will smell me coming." she said

"Well, no. This is the one of the cool things about this shi---stuff." I said, with unhidden excitement. "It doesn't work on Lore. It's specifically made to work only for humans."

"Ohh, this I gotta see." Rail said, taking the spray can.

She aimed it at me and I quickly took it out of her hands. Rail had a puzzled look on her face as I looked at Danion not wanting to explain myself.

"Take my word for it. It works." I said. "If you didn't have eyes or ears you wouldn't know a human was right next to you with this stuff."

"Sage..." Danion said. "You say this spray blocks the human scent from Lore. Does that mean if a Lore was in a room full of humans and then sprayed themselves with this would other Lore be about to smell those humans on that Lore?"

"Maybe. Hell, probably paranoid as the Quinns are. Kill a Lore then spray the area so you can't track 'em back home. Probably best against werewolves since they're the best trackers."

Danion put his hands over his face, paced the room, then slammed his fist to the wall.

"Damn it." he cried. "I knew they were hiding something. 'Knew they weren't telling me everything."

He was ranking and mostly talking to himself. Rail and I looked at him only getting bits of what he was saying.

"What those Quinns said last night... I couldn't believe it. But they spray proof everything." he said. "And they knew. They knew."

Rail and I looked back at each other and asked the obvious question, "They who?"

He looked back at us quietly and hesitant to say anything but then answered.

"The Consortia." he said.

"Ahh, shit." said Rail.

Me? I spun aimlessly in my chair hoping I that didn't hear what I heard.

"I should have told you this, I know but---"

"You think?" I said, cutting him off. "Hey... there's my phone. Why don't you call 109 so everybody knows where I live, damn it! Alright, I want the whole story... from the beginning."

Danion told us how the Consortia wanted him to find the snitch that was selling out the Lore and that all the evidence was leading to one un-escapable conclusion.

"The snitch is Lore." he said.

"Are you crazy?" said Rail. "No Lore would sell out another to the Quinns."

"It's happened before." said Danion.

"Yeah and after the Consortia was through it never happened again." I said. "I can't believe you're working for them again."

Danion just looked at me giving an explanation in silence.

And I finally got it.

"This is about '91, isn't it?" I asked him.

"It will be number two if I find the snitch." he said.

"Give me an hour." I said. "Maybe I can help."

"What happened in '91?" Rail asked.

"I did something that exposed the Lore." he said. "The Consortia covered it up but still wasn't happy. So, they 'offered' me a deal. I do three tasks for them and they forget what I did. I don't like working for them but they're right. We have to stop the snitch before another Lore gets hit like you and those trolls."

"Trolls?" she asked.

"Yeah, the Quinns took out a pit last night before everything went to hell."

Rail's mind immediately flashed back to where Sal said Kyle was the two days after the Quinn attack.

"I know who it is." she said. "I know who ratting us out, damn it! It's Kyle!"

"Who?"

Rail told Danion about Kyle leaving her behind and where he was before Kyle came back. Danion literally had to stand in front of the door and hold her arms to keep Rail from running back to the Breakers and killing him.

"Wait." he said. "Think about it. You don't have any proof."

"Are you deaf? What did I just tell you." she said "The fight with the Brood---Now that I think about it... he kept pushing for that fight since day one. To get us all in a nice little bunch. Sonavabitch!"

"Alright from your point of view it could be him." Danion said. "But without proof it'll just look like you're trying to get back at him for the park."

With a growl she turned away. Pissed off but knowing Danion was right.

"So, what do we do?" Rail asked.

"Watch him. Find out if he's really the snitch. Then...'deal with him.'"

"'Deal with him?'" she asked, knowing full well what it meant.

And smiling about it.

"Well, that's what the kids are calling it but that's only if he's the one." said Danion.

Some time passed and neither one said much. Rail paced the room in frustration. Knowing what Kyle had done and not being able to choke the life out of him made her vent more with each step. She folded her arms trying to think of her next move while causally glancing over to Danion, who was looking on me wondering what I was doing in the lab. Her glance turned into a full-on stare as she slightly bit her bottom lip and rose an eyebrow to the sight of Danion's backside.

"What it is?" he asked, catching her staring but not knowing where she was staring.

"What?" she cried, snapping out of her stare.

"You were staring."

"No, I wasn't. I was... thinking. I stare when I think." she insisted, quickly turning her head away.

She looked and found that she was facing a glass frame picture and that the reflecting glass was showing her blushing face. Rail wasn't about to turn back around so she hid her face away from Danion. Who knows how long that would had been if I didn't finish my ump-teenth good deed of the century for Danion.

"Better get in here." I said. "You two are going to love this."

They immediately smelled something foul when they came into the lab.

"What's that smell?" asked Rail.

"Good. It's working." I said.

"What?" asked Danion.

"My little concoction." I proudly boasted holding up a beaker of blue liquid.

I laid out a paper napkin and sprayed the Quinns' spray on it.

"Hold your nose." I said, putting a drop of the 'blue' on the same napkin.

Suddenly that foul smell came from the napkin.

"Put this stuff on anything the 'cover' spray is on and it will reek to high heaven. Burns a little, too" I said, rubbing my hand.

"Yes! Thank-you." Rail cried, taking the beaker.

"Hey." I said

"She thinks she has a line on the snitch." said Danion.

"Really? Who?" I asked

"An asshole and I need this to prove it." she said.

"Fine... but there's an empty spray bottle in the bottom cabaret." I pointed. "It will work a lot better."

As she went to get the bottle, I told Danion if he ever ran into the Quinns again, which was more than likely, he could use my spray to track them to their base. With that smell it would be easy. He agreed it was a good idea then went quiet when he caught the tattoo on the small of Rail's back as she was bending down to get that spray bottle. He actually angled his head to try to see pass down the tattoo. That is until I caught what he was doing and started giggling like a five-year-old.

"Shut-up." he told me.

"What?" Rail asked.

"Nothing." I said, still snickering a bit.

Rail gave me the spray bottle so I could pour the blue into it.

"We need to get together later." Danion told her.

"Why?" she asked, on the edge of blushing again.

"So... you can tell me if this Kyle's the snitch."

"Yeah, right.... obviously." she said, relieved that her face wasn't going to turn red.

"We'll meet on the roof where we..."

His mind flashed on the kiss on that roof but Danion wasn't going to say the word 'Kiss'. Not in front of me and not in front of her. Luckily Rail filled in the blank.

"Where we landed after the Quinns." she said.

"Yeah... that's good. 9:00?" he asked.

"Nine will be fine."

"It's a date." I said, giving Rail the spray bottle.

"Shut up." they both told me.

They looked at each other saying to themselves 'Please don't let her/him think this is a date'.

In fact, they insisted on it.

"It's not a date." they said.

Rail walked into the Breakers' hangout and was welcome by Sal.

"Where have you been?" Sal asked, in that suspicious tone.

"Out."

"Where and with whom?"

"Suspicious, aren't we? Where's Kyle I wanna talk to him." said Rail.

"Why?" Sal said with a worried tone.

"I just need to talk to him." she said, eager to down to business.

Sal went over to Rail and carefully padded her down.

"Just checking for weapons." said Sal. "What this?"

Sal was holding the spray bottle in front of Rail. She couldn't have told Sal the truth so she said the first time that she thought Sal would believe.

"Body spray." she said.

Rail immediately rolled her eyes to that answer. There was no way Sal was going to believe that she would have something so frilly. Sal looked at the bottle and then at Rail and started giggling.

"What... you trying to smell nice for your little vampire?" she smiled.

"Shut-up." Rail cried, trying to snatch the spray but missing.

"Kiddin'. But seriously it's good you talking to Kyle. Work things out."

"Oh... I plan to."

"Good" Sal said, causally spraying herself. "Everyone needs a little forgiv..."

Suddenly it hit them both like a wave.

The smell.

"Ohhh... my Goddess." Sal said.

"What is this stuff?! It smells...and it's-It's burning me!"

Sal started rapidly slapping her hands to get rid of the burn sensation.

 Rail?

She just stared at her friend.

Her best friend.

Not even wanting to conceive what this could mean.

"Rail... where did you get this crap?!" Sal screamed.

"Rail! Rail?! Why are you staring at me like that?"

4

You know the thing about Rail is that she would do anything for a friend. It's not just her inherent werewolf loyalty but It's her. The way she is and her willingness to go to hell and back for someone she cares about. Yeah... there's no doubt she'll fight, kill, and sacrifice for a friend. Sal was a friend. The same friend who Rail found out was selling out the Lore to the Quinns... and who because of this Rail was once again staring at the barrel of a gun loaded with silver bullets.

At least this Quinn wasn't like the last one. He didn't enjoy killing but was firmly committed that he was doing the Lord's work.

Which made him even more dangerous.

"May God have mercy on your immortal soul." the Quinn said to her.

He took aim and fired three times into the center of Rail's chest. She laid on the ground in stillness as her body slowly reverted back to human form. Her yellow eyes returned to the color of Caribbean-blue which faded into darkness as her eyelids fell shut.

Wondering how the hell this happened?

Good question.

It was 9:17 in the PM, when Rail finally arrived on the roof. Obviously tense but not wanting Danion to see it she played it calm and cool.

"Your late." he said.

"Yeah... uh sorry."

"Well?"

"Well, what?" she asked.

"Is Kyle the snitch?"

"Kyle? No...no, he's not the snitch."

"But you seemed so positive befor---"

"It's not him!" she yelled. "I practically dumped the whole bottle on him. No smell. It's-not-him, damn it!"

Danion was perplexed by her tone wondering what 'that' was all about then guess Rail was angry that Kyle wasn't the snitch. Which was half true.

"Okay." he said, in a calmer tone to not upset her anymore.

"I guess we're back to square one."

"We? No. There is no 'we' here." she pointed out. "The Consortia wanted you to find this snitch. I thought I knew who it was. I was wrong. I'm out. That's it. Finished. Through."

Danion saw that look of conviction and acknowledged it with a nod.

"Fine. So, I guess this is the last time we'll see each other?" he said.

Rail was silent for a moment at that thought.

"Yeah, pretty much." she said.

Again, Danion nodded and was about to take off when Rail stopped him.

"Wait." she said. "You said a Lore did this before. What happened exactly to him...or her".

"Why?"

"Just wondering what happened?"

"I wasn't there personally." he said. "But from what I've heard over the years... it wasn't pretty."

Rail listened as Danion told her the story of two vampires. What they were fighting about no one really knows. But one just got fed up and secretly told the Quinns about the other. The Quinns killed the Vampire and a month later the Consortia picked up the other one.

Now, this is the part were most Lore have exaggerated, build up, or made up like a lot of legends and myths. But then again, a lot of legends and myths have some small truth to them.

The most popular version is that the Consortia ordered 100 Lore to a secret underground cavern. There they laid the vampire in a Christ-like position. They used the ancient Chinese water torture but the drops of water that hit his head were holy. It wasn't enough to kill him but it did melt a hole through his skull. It's also said they didn't limit this torture to only one 'head' to his body. They then cut open his chest from the bottom of his neck passed his stomach. Pulling back his skin they placed tiny crosses on his internal organs. Lungs. Liver. Kidneys. As for the heart they took tiny wooden splinters and put them throughout his heart. Still not enough to kill him but the pain was immense. His hands and feet were set on fire with a slow burning compound. It lasted for hours. Then they placed a steel or wooden sheet over him with pin-holes letting the sunlight burn him but not engulf him. How he got burned underground? Who knows? There has been so many telling of this story but one clear point that everybody seems to agree on is before the vampire was finally killed the Consortia announced that the vampire was the second most miserable creature on the face of the earth. The first... would be the one who ever did anything like that again. Well, that was it. Word spread. The Consortia became a force to be very feared and the Lore, though many of them still had long standing feuds, never betrayed another to the Quinns...

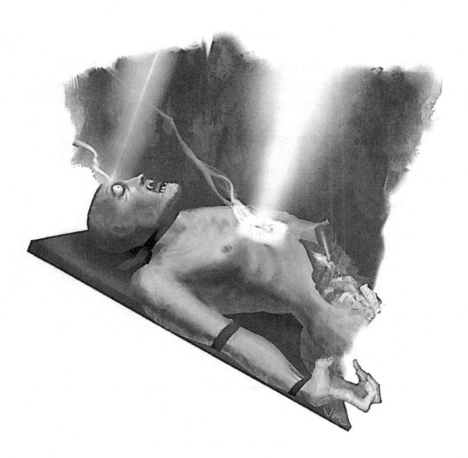

Until now.

"So, what do you think they'll do now?" Rail asked.

"I don't know."

"Well you said you were going to 'deal with it'"

"I don't know who or what I'm dealing with." he said. "More than likely they'll show up and 'deal with it'."

"How?"

"Honestly... I really don't want to know."

With that he took off into the air leaving Rail to run back to the hangout and Sal. She didn't waste any time in ransacking through Sal's stuff until she found the Quinn cover spray.

What the hell are you doing?" cried Sal, finding Rail

"You're working for the Quinns." said Rail.

"W-What?" Sal said, with a half giggle.

"You're working for the Quinns." Rail repeated this facing time her.

"Rail... if this is a joke it's really---"

"That shit that was reeking off you."

"Yeah, I was in the shower for an hou---"

"It's only smells when it's mixed with this!" she yelled, holding the cover spray up.

Sal's eyes became fixed on the sight of the spray can.

"What's that?" Sal asked.

"Oh, god don't play the idiot on me, Sal! This blocks the scent of humans from us. That's why you have it so we wouldn't know that you're working with the Quinns!"

"I'm not with the Quinns." Sal said, in a cold stare.

"You've been selling us out... why?"

"I am not with the Quinns."

Sick of her lying mouth Rail transformed and pinned Sal to the wall by the neck with her elbow.

"Stop lying to me, damn it!" Rail screamed. "Say it! Say you're with the Quinns!"

Suddenly a burst of adrenaline went through Sal as she transformed and pushed Rail across the room.

"I-AM-NOT-WITH-THE-QUINNS, DAMN, IT!" she yelled to the top of her lungs.

Before Rail could react Sal was on her with her claws around Rail's throat.

"They have my brother." Sal said, turning back into human form. "They have my brother and nephew."

Sal knees collapsed under her. She fell to the floor into the fetal position saying over again, 'Goddess, please help me. Goddess, please help me.' Rail just looked at Sal with her anger and rage replaced by empathy and compassion as she took hold of her friend trying to ease her pain.

The other Breakers started showing up wondering what was going on. Rail responded by telling them to 'Get the hell out!'

"Please tell me what the hell is going on." Rail asked her.

Sal nodding her head relieved that she could finally talk about it.

"Not here, though." Rail said. "Someplace where they can't hear through the wall."

They were out the door and in a few minutes in an alley behind a fast food joint.

"Talk to me." said Rail.

Sal didn't know where to start because she didn't know exactly how it started.

"A couple months ago I got a phone call. A guy named Michaels wanted to talk about to me about my brother, Paul." Sal said. "So, naturally-stupidly I go. As soon as I met him he tells me he's knows what I am and if I want to see my brother and nephew again, I need give up Lore for the Quinns."

At first Sal didn't believe Michaels. That is until he gave her a cellphone and found out from Paul that he and his son were under Quinn 'protection'. If she did what the Quinns said they'll be safe.

"And you believed them?" Rail asked, shaking her head. "Hello? Quinns. Dedicated to destroying us. It's been two months how do you know your brother and nephew are still alive.

"They're alive." Sal said to convince herself more than Rail. "I've talked to them. He's given me stuff with a fresh scent on it. Beside the Quinns won't hurt them their...'

"They're what?"

"They're... human."

Well, Rail was dumb-strucked. She knew Sal had a brother and nephew, but just assumed they were werewolves, too.

"After my folks broke up my mother hooked-up with a human." Sal said. "Nine months later Paul came out but he was human... and so is Kenny."

Surprised? Don't be. With Humans and Lore being on the same planet for so long there was bound to be some fraternization. And the offspring of those unions? Sometimes they're Lore. Sometimes they're humans. Sometimes they're a little of both. Ever seen anybody with rubber band arms who's stronger than a weightlifter. Someone with one or two enhance senses. That guy who always seems to knows what other people are feeling. That girl who's really good with every kind of animal. And of course, the ever-popular longevity. You know those people in their 60's who look 40.

Yeah, I know who you are... Lynda Carter.

"I didn't know what to do." Sal said. "It was just vampires at first. Didn't feel bad about vampires but Michaels wanted more. He wanted variety to make sure they were getting us all. Demons. Gargoyles. Trolls."

'Trolls?" Rail asked sparking curiosity. "How did you know about the trolls under the bridge? 'Cause from my timetable didn't Kyle tell you after the Quinn attack?"

"When we were clubbing for those two days for Mic and the others. I heard a troll say that a werewolf was hiding out with his cousin after a Quinn attack. I knew it was Kyle but Michaels demanded another lead. I didn't even try to save him."

"How did this Michaels even find out about you?"

"How." Sal said. "Because... were related."

With a stunned expression Rail asked the obvious question of 'How?'.

"My brother's wife, Emily."

"The one who die." said Rail.

"Yeah... a couple of years ago." said Sal. "I went to visit Paul six months ago for Kenny's birthday but I wasn't the only relative there. Emily's uncle showed up... Father Jacob Michaels."

Rail shook her head in disbelief.

"I didn't know he was a Quinn so I wasn't that careful" Sal said, feeling so stupid. "My brother lives in a small house near the woods. One night I got a little nostalgic and..."

"Went trumping through the woods." said Rail. "Everybody does that."

"Well, Michaels must have saw and hatched this whole thing up."

"Perfect. Just... perfect." Rail said, putting her hand over her face.

The two just stood there not saying anything and wondering what to do next until Sal broke the silence with a four-word statement that needed and wanted to be said.

"I didn't do it." she said.

"Do what?" Rail asked.

"I saw your eyes when I said 'Mic and the others'." Sal said. "I didn't tell the Quinns about us in the park. I was surprised as anybody when they came over that hill."

"I know."

"Do you?" Sal asked, not convinced.

"I doubt you'd call the Quinns to hit us with you there." Rail said. "I also don't think you would carry me to safety, been ready to take on Quinns, and refuse to leave me if you set us up to die."

"T-Thank-you." Sal said, close to tears and grateful that Rail believed her when probably no one else would. "But I'm still in deep, aren't I?"

"Yeah. First thing we need to do is get your brother and nephew away from the Quinns."

"Don't you think I know that!" Sal cried. "I thought I could track them one time but Michaels keeps using that damn spray on me. Besides, I think they keep moving them. When I talk to them on the phone the background always sounds different."

"Then we have to think of something else." said Rail.

"That would be my guess." said Danion.

The two were shocked, especially Rail to see Danion in the alley with them.

"What are you doing here?" cried Rail.

"Who's this?" asked Sal.

"Vampire." Rail said worried.

"'Your' vampire?" she asked.

"Stay away from her!" Rail ordered Danion.

"What's going on?" Sal asked in a worried tone.

"The Consortia sent him." said Rail.

"The Consortia." she said, with fear aimed at Danion.

"Wait." Rail said. "You don't understand. They're forcing her."

"I know." he said "I heard everything."

"But you don't care, right?" Rail said. "What are you going to do to her."

"I'm not going to do anything." said Danion.

"You're lying." cried Rail. "Run Sal!"

"Do-not-run." Danion told Sal. "Run and they will find you."

Sal looked at Danion, stood up tall, and slowly walked towards him

"You're right." she said calmly. "I won't run."

At first, Rail thought Danion was hypnotizing her but then remembered vampires can't do that to werewolves. Sal was doing it on her own free will. She stopped short from him as Rail stuck her arm out between them to make sure Danion didn't try anything.

"You're a traitor." he said to Sal.

"Yes." Sal said with no denial.

"Lore are dead because of you." he said.

"Yes." Sal said with clear guilt.

"Do you have any idea what the Consortia will do to you?" he asked.

"Everything I probably deserved." said Sal.

"When's your next meeting with Michaels?" he asked Sal.

"Midnight tonight." she said, fully expecting not to make the meeting.

"It's 10:27 now." Danion said, looking at his watch. "That means we have about an hour and a half to figure out something...that hopefully won't get us all killed."

It was earlier that day at 5 0'clock in the PM that the Quinns were 'protecting' Sal's brother and nephew in an out of the way Motel 6. In the last two month they were moved at least once a week around Denver.

Kenny really didn't know what was going on. He was the kind of kid who could have an adventure with a large cardboard box. His father on the other hand knew exactly why they were there. They were prisoners. He saw lots of opportunities to escape but was worried about the repercussions. Mostly towards his sister, Sal. He constantly thought about two months ago when Father Michaels showed up at the front door. He naturally opened up his home for family only to find this relative was kidnapping him and his son as bargaining chips. The last time he talked to Sal Paul knew that the pressure was getting to her but he didn't know the city, or where Sal was, and he certainly couldn't go to the police. So, he and his son were as trap as his sister.

"So, how is everyone?" Michaels smiled, as he came through the motel door.

"Uncle Mikey! Uncle Mikey!" Kenny cried, jumping into his uncle's arms.

"How have you been Kenneth?" asked his uncle.

"This place is getting boring." Kenny said.

"Well... we'll have to change that, won't we?"

"So... we're moving again?" asked Paul.

"Yes, we are and Kenneth is going to love it." Michaels said. "Now get packed. It's a big surprise."

Kenny, faster than a bolt went to get his stuff while Michaels walked Paul outside to talk privately.

"Where are we going now?" Paul asked.

"Like I said it's a surprise" he smiled.

"Paul just wanted to smack that smile off Michaels' face but resisted the temptation for an answer to a question.

"When is this going to end?"

"Hopefully never." said Michaels.

"Do you have any idea what they'll do to her if she's found out?" Paul asked, looking for some kind of compassion in Michaels.

"Yes...and the loss of your sister... as a source would be tragic for the cause."

"The cause? Screw your cause!" Paul yelled. "This is my sister we're talking about here. Why are you doing this?"

"Because Paul the Lord has given us an opportunity. One that probably won't come again for a very long time. And I plan to use it to its fullest extent." Michaels said. "By any means necessary."

"By any means necessary? So, what happens with us and your God Squad. I am half wolf you know."

"You and Kenneth are both human by the grace of God. The abomination that is your sister---"

"She is not an abomination!" Paul cried, grabbing Michaels by the collar. "Next to Emily she is the kindest person I've ever know."

"Yet, she betrays her own." said Michaels. "As for you and Kenneth everybody knows the truth."

"They do?"

"Yes… I told them that you knew the identity of the abomination. And that you have been brought here to be protected because you know it's secret."

"Protected? From Sal?" Paul said, hearing the most ridiculous thing.

"Yes." Michaels pointed out. "If she betrays her own kind to protect you, how long will it be before she betrays you to protect herself?"

Michaels turned to go back to the motel room leaving Paul in disbelief about his last statement.

Then again… fanatics can reason anything to their philosophy.

Time was running out for Rail, Danion, and Sal's plan. Three guesses to where they plotted their little scheme and they all start with my place. Again… needless to say. I found their plan lacking a few points.

"Like what?" Rail asked.

"One, you don't know where the Quinns are stashing her kin." I said. "Two, you don't know how many Quinns will be there and after your little warehouse fiasco I would think beefing up security would be a big priority for them. Three, and this is just my personal opinion... this is frickin' nuts!"

"We stay low and out of sight it could work, Sage" Danion told me.

"Famous last words, kid." I told him.

"It would probably work a lot better if we had a little more help." he said.

He looked at me. They all looked at me. Like I wasn't getting it, duh?

"Ohh... do not pull me into this. Hey, I feel for you." I said to Sal. "But even if you could by some miracle pull this off... you still have the Consortia to deal with."

They all went quiet. Seems they all forgotten that little point.

"We'll cross that bridge later." said Danion.

"This plan just gets more brilliant by the moment." I said.

"What choice do we have?" asked Sal.

I looked at them and knew they were going to do this.

Well, of course they were it's the climax to this story.

"Well... if you're that determine" I said shaking my head. "Maybe I got a thing or two that can help."

Phase one of the plan. Get Michaels to take Sal to her kin that night and follow them by air. Problem. Michaels probably wouldn't go for it (you think?). So, the question was how they were going get him to go for it?

We'll the truth sometimes help.

"You're late." Michaels said to Sal.

"There's a problem. The Consortia on to me." Sal said. "They sent someone after me."

"Please don't try to fool me with the myth of the Consortia."

"You don't believe in the Consortia?"

"The Consortia." he answered with a snicker. "The abomination's great protector. Yet this group has never attacked us... your greatest threat."

"Whether or not you believe in the Consortia it doesn't matter. I need to see my brother."

"Why?"

"'Cause they're going to kill me your dumbass!" she cried. "And I want to see Paul and Kenny before that happens."

"And then make some kind of daring escape. I don't think so."

Sal showed her yellow eyes and fangs teeth in intimidation.

It wasn't working.

"If you kill me you will never see Paul and Kenneth again." Michaels pointed out. "So... please stop the theatrics and tell me what you have for us tonight."

"Not till I see my brother and Kenny, damn it."

"No."

"Then you don't get the Drac-cul." she said.

"A Drac-cul? Here? "Michaels asked.

"Only tonight. Gone by tomorrow."

"Where?"

She didn't answer.

Remember when I told you there were different kinds of vampires. Well, the Drac-cul are the top of the line. Hell, they're above it. Can't get into detail right now but let's just say there's no Quinn that wouldn't give their high teeth to bag one.

Which was why Michaels agreed to Sal's terms.

She was blindfolded all the way there. When it was taken off Michaels lead her though a building. They passed at least ten Quinns when she realized something was wrong and then it came to her.

"They don't know." she said.

"Know what?" he asked.

"That I'm the one who's been given you information. They don't know that I'm a Lore, do they?"

"I suggest you keep that to yourself." Michaels said. "For everybody's sake."

"What? Father Michaels doesn't want the God Squad knowing his kin to Lore?"

"We are not 'kin' in anyway." he stressed. "Now, where's the Drac-cul."

"Where's my brother and Kenny?"

He led her to a door and behind it she was greeted by her brother's smile.

"Hey." she said, giving her Paul a huge hug. "Where's Kenny?"

"Sleeping in the next room." Paul motioned his head. "You okay?"

"I could do better." she said, looking at Michaels then telling him that she wanted to be alone with Paul.

"Fine." Michaels said. "You have five minutes then I want that information."

He left and Sal and Paul looked at each other examining their situation.

"So how bad is it?" he asked.

"Maybe not as bad as you think, Pauly."

Paul recognized the tone of hope in her voice.

"You got something up your sleeve?" he hoped.

"More in my ear." she said, pushing her hair back to show her ear-mic.

Brotherhood.

It was one of the many old ghost towns in Colorado. Except in the fifties a money man decided to turn it into a tourist attraction. Rebuild to the modern codes of the time it had water, power, and a year from opening until the money man filed for bankruptcy. But the Quinns and their deep pockets bought the town and the land around it for a base of operations. It was perfect with it just an hour outside Denver, tons of space for training, privacy, and located where the Quinns could see anything coming at them.

Well... almost anything.

Rail and Danion looked over the old western town. The mic in Sal's ear also doubled as a homing device. Hey, it's the 21st century. They landed on a small cliff that gave a great view of Brotherhood. Danion had to carry Rail in his arms for the entire trip. Neither of them minded, in fact Rail loved it now that she had the time to appreciate it. She had to wrap her arms tightly around Danion so she wouldn't fall. Though a little embarrassed it wasn't the only reason she was holding on so tight.

When Michaels took Sal to Brotherhood Rail asked Danion how they were going to follow.

He pointed up.

"We're gonna fly?" she asked, with hidden excitement.

"You're not afraid of highs, are you?"

She was going to say a flat 'No' but something inside of her made her say something else.

"A little." she lied.

"Just hang on tight." he said, picking her up in his arms. "Don't worry. I won't let you fall."

So that's what she did. Wrapped her arms around him... tight.

"Doesn't look hard." Rail said, looking down at Brotherhood.

"Looks can be deceiving."

"Okay... let's do it."

"Hold it, Xena." he said "We wait to see if 'Phase Two' pans out."

"Think they'll go for it?" Rail asked.

"A Drac-cul." Danion said, with a chuckled. "Oh, yeah."

"Are so many needed?" Michaels asked SL, who was overseeing the mobilization for the Drac-cul strike

"I'm wondering if we have enough." SL said. "The files on Drac-culs are sketchy at best. Only that they're very powerful, hard to kill, and often use other abominations as a security force. Speaking of security... I heard you breached it by bring an outsider here."

"It's---she's my nephew-in-law's sister." Michaels said, catching himself. "She was worried. They've talked over the phone but she needed to see him to know he was safe."

"What did you tell her about us?"

"The truth."

"And she believed it?" SL asked.

"You find that she very accepting to the shadow world that inhabits ours." Michaels said. "But you seem worried."

"Her? No. But who knows what we're going to face here."

"God is with us. Said Michaels. "There is nothing to fear."

"That's not what I'm worried about. I just don't like going into a situation where I don't have all the intel. The source didn't give you anything other than the Drac-cul's location?" the SL asked.

"Sh---it was lucky it got that much. The Drac-cul are so secretive and paranoid that they're nearly impossible to track down."

"So, we have to move quickly." SL said. "Oh, and about the sister..."

"Don't worry, she's no threat." Michaels said, secretly padding the gun under his coat. "I'll make sure of it."

Rail and Danion watched as the Quinn caravan headed to the city to fight a Drac-cul that wasn't there. Sighs and hope went through them as they realized that Phase Two was panning out by getting as many Quinns away from their base as possible.

"They're leaving. She did it." Rail said.

"Yeah, now let's give it some time." he said.

"Why?"

"Because I really doubt it's going to be a cakewalk down there. And if the Quinns call for reinforcement the farther away they are the better it is for us."

Rail saw the logic in that and also wanted to take the opportunity (just in case there wasn't on later) to say something.

"Thank-you for doing this." she said.

"Well, Sal's not the first one to do what she did to save a loved one. I've seen it before. Good and honest people like her. Then someone comes alone and uses their family against them. It's not an excuse for what she done... she knows that, but I can understand her explanation." he said

"Hey... how did you know I was lying to you on the roof?" she asked.

"The Consortia story." Danion started. "I've never known a werewolf not to smile, giggle, or laugh out loud hearing that story. You did none of those things... so I got suspicious."

"And you followed me."

"To your place then the alley."

Rail shook her head thinking she probably would have smelled him if she wasn't preoccupied with Sal. Then something popped in her head.

"What about the Consort---"

"We'll deal with that later..." he said. "If there is a later."

"Well, thank-you... again." she said. "For this and... saving me from the Quinn that first night."

"You're welcome. And thank-you for saving me from those two Quinns at the warehouse. And... you're probably right."

"About?"

"They could probably count them as two separate saves."

Hearing that made Rail smile.

"Now, I have a question." Danion asked.

"Yeah?"

"Back in the alley what did Sal mean by 'your vampire'?

Rail's smile went away in hopes that she wasn't blushing again.

It was time.

An hour had passed and 'Phase Three' of the plan seemed simple. Cause a distraction that leads the Quinns away so that Sal and her kin could have a clear path of escape... but as the old saying goes, 'The best laid plans.'

They landed just outside of town both going into lurking mode. The large area and many alleys between buildings made it easy to avoid the Quinns until they had to separate.

"Okay, I'll find the main power source to this place and take it out." Danion said. "You smell out Sal and help her get pass the Quinns."

"Alright." she said, sniffing the air. "Got her."

She looked at Danion and got a little worried. Rail started to reach out her hand to his face but at the last second softly punched his shoulder.

"Be careful." she said, running off.

"I will." he said. "You, too."

He found the powerhouse pretty easily behind another building. There were only two Quinns protecting it outside and in. Danion made short work of them. They weren't dead but they weren't conscious either. Inside it was exactly liked he hoped in one big switch to turn off the power. He grabbed it, pulled it, and watts of searing pain went through his body throwing him across the room. He was already out cold before he hit the floor and the Quinns surrounded him.

"He's out." one Quinn said. "Better finish him off."

The Quinn pulled out a stake and aimed it over Danion's heart.

"No." another said. "Take him out back and chain him up. I gotta better idea."

Rail followed the scent of Sal to a saloon/dancehall building. She was across the street telling Sal through the ear-mic to get ready to move when she heard someone behind her. Immediately, she moved and elbowed a Quinn disarming him. When she saw the others about to fire their weapons Rail transformed and used the first Quinn as a body-shield and battering ram. Bullets went into Quinn killing him as the two other Quinns were knocked to the ground by Rail. She then took a good sniff in the air and smell nothing from the Quinns.

"I may not be able to smell you assholes but I can hear you coming a mile awa---"

Suddenly her body was shocked with pain. Rail fell forward revealing two electrical wires in her back that were connected to a taser. Her body numb she could barely turn around to face her attacker. All she saw was the gun.

'May God have mercy on your immortal soul.' was all Rail heard before the pain of three silver bullets were fired into her chest.

"Rail. Rail!" Sal said, into her ear-mic but getting no response.

"What's wrong?" Paul asked.

"I-I don't know. We were talking then I heard fighting and gunshots." she said.

The door opened and Michaels came in to talk to Sal.

"Very clever but it didn't work." he said.

"What didn't work?" she asked in fear.

Michaels pulled back the window curtains and Sal screamed at the sight of Rail's body on the street.

"What have you done?!" she cried.

"Cleansed the world of yet another abomination." Michaels said.

"You sonavabitch!" she yelled, transforming and wrapping her claw around his throat.

"What's going on?" said a sleepy Kenny coming out of the next room rubbing his eyes.

Sal quickly turned back to her human form to greet her nephew.

"Hey honey." she said, with tears in her eyes.

"Aunt Sally! Aunt Sally!" he said, rushing into her arms then noticing her tears. "You're crying."

"I'm just... really happy to see you." she said, giving Kenny a big hug.

"I want to talk to you in ten minutes." Michaels said, leaving the room.

Sal didn't say anything but knew she didn't have a choice. Her brother came and hugged her as she hugged Kenny to comfort her pain. Rail was dead she told herself. Michaels was on to her and Rail's vampire... wait. What happened to the vampire?

A wave of cold water splashed across Danion face reviving him. He looked around with water still dripping from his eyes barely focusing on the three Quinns in front of him. He got to his feet and found that his arms were chained to the ground. He froze in a dead stare looking at the iron around wrist. The sounds of their clanging made his mind flashback to a time when chains and black people where an all too common place. More to the point... chains on black people.

"No... Get-them... off me." he said. "Get them off me now! Not this. Not this. I'm not going through this again. Never again!"

He kept ranting continuously until he was shocked to the ground by a cattle-prod. Danion cried in pain as the Quinns gave him another jolt for good measure smiling over their capture.

"That took the fight out of him." One of the Quinns said.

"Think it's still conscious, though." another said, snapping his fingers at Danion.

"Good... want it wide and awake when the sun comes up." said the third Quinn.

The Sun.

Danion' eyes widen at the word.

"How long we got?" The first Quinn asked.

"A little over three hours." the third Quinn said, looking at his watch.

"Hey... I think this is the same one from the warehouse." the second Quinn said, hitting Danion with the cattle-prod again.

Danion laid on the ground feeling the pain of the prod but still having enough strength to start wrapping the chain around his right arm and hand.

"Probably the same fleabag, too?" said the third Quinn.

"Yeah, but those three slugs of silver took care of her." said the first Quinn. "Hear that? Your little dog is dead."

"She's-no-dog." said Danion, with red glowing eyes.

With a primal yell he broke the chain on his right arm breaking his hand in the process from the force of pulling that chain. He hit the second Quinn with the cattle-prod across the jaw. The chain around Danion's hand worked like brass knuckles. That mixed with a lot of vampire strength made the Quinn go flying. Before the other two could react Danion pulled the spike out of the ground that was chaining his left side. It was four feet long and more than perfect to impale both Quinns through the chest. Not one at a time but both men at once. He lifted both of them in the air and watched happily as their life's blood left their bodies and covered the spike.

He dropped them on the ground and started to head towards the Quinn he first hit but was held back by the chain that was still attached to the spike that was still inside the Quinns.

Danion found the key on one of the dead Quinns and freed himself to deal with the last one. He picked the Quinn up by the collar and saw the cattle-prod on the ground. He wanted to use it but Danion had a better idea for this particular Quinn... since they had the same skin color.

"You put chains on me. On me. Do you have any idea the hypocrisy in that? I've been a vampire for nearly 200 years. Before that I was human. Black, human, and living in America. I'm sure you know history surrounding those facts. Now, don't say you understand, 'cause you cannot understand. What? Old ladies crossing the street when they see you? Being followed in the mall? Cops pulling you over 'cause you're not driving the right type of car for your complexion. Try your eye being burned out because you know your A-B-C's. Or being whipped because you looked at some guy in the eye by mistake. Or never seeing your little sister again because your mas... the guy who owns her lost a poker hand! I know you can't possibly understand these things but don't worry... you will" Danion said, sinking his fangs into the Quinn's neck.

They say when a vampire feed, the victim and them become one sharing memories and consciousness. In an instant Danion knew the past of the Quinn. His first kiss. His football days. The day he joined the Quinns. And in turn the Quinn knew Danion's past. The memories always faded fast once the feeding was over but before that happened there was just enough time... even through a broken jaw for the Quinn to say two words.

"I'm sorry." he said falling to die.

"I sure you are." Danion said, wiping the blood off his month.

His broken hand was rapidly healing thanks to the shot of blood. Danion looked around at the dead Quinns and smiled at his victory. Then closed his eyes in the reality it was a hollow victory.

"She's dead." he told himself. "She dead."

The two Quinns that Rail knocked around earlier were now carrying her body to an empty room.

"I don't know why Michaels wants to bury this thing." one Quinn said, dropping Rail on the floor.

"Its' curse is over." the other said. "It... she deserves a chance to be with God."

"Well, God's going to be sending that vamp flaming back to hell when the sun comes up."

"Should be interesting to see."

"You don't know the half of it." the first Quinn said. "First they start to smoke then they catch fire. Sometimes they burn slowly. Sometimes they burn fast. Other times they just explode."

"You enjoy this way too much. Come on... let's patch you up. You're starting to bleed behind your ear."

Suddenly it just hit the second Quinn.

"Bleeding?" he said, tuning around. "Waitamiu---"

Before the Quinn could finish his sentence, a razor-sharp claw went into both Quinns. When the claws pulled out of their bodies they were covered in blood and shreds of internal organs. The Quinns' dead bodies fell to the floor leaving Rail standing over them. She stumbled to the floor still feeling the pain of those three slugs, but then smiled over what the alternative could have been if it wasn't for my tiny gift of a bullet-proof vest. I said I had a thing or two that could help. A werewolf going to a Quinn stronghold? It just made sense. Too bad it didn't do the same for tasers. When she was shocked and shot, she could have tried to get up but with more Quinns coming she decided to play dead and hoped no one noticed. Obviously, something went wrong. She was found too easily and the power was still on. Then Rail remembered what those Quinns said about 'the vamp' and 'the sun' and immediately bolted out the room because of it.

Sal was led to Michaels' office still crying over seeing what she thought was Rail's death.

"Very well... let's cut to the chase." he said. "Obviously your Drac-cul lead was a lie so your friends could help you escape with your brother and Kenneth."

"How did you find out?" she asked, shaking her head on how bad things went.

Michaels explained that though the Quinns use classic methods to kill the abominations. It was the 21st century. He told her about the small radar dish on top of the building that picks up anything flying in their airspace that's smaller than a plane and bigger than a bird. There were motion/heat detectors all over the less traveled parts of Brotherhood. When 'something' is not supposed to be there the troops are sent in. They knew that at least one was a vampire because there was movement but no heat (vampires don't give off body heat). They knew he was heading to the powerhouse and let him. Anyone who was going to attack the Quinns would want to knock out the power first, so they booby-trap it with a single ON/OFF switch which didn't control the power at all. It just electrocutes the target and that's how they caught Danion.

"What have you done with him?" she asked.

"The sun will purify him in the morning." said Michaels. "And your friend will also be buried in the morning. Now that her cursed is over she deserves a proper burial."

"We're not cursed!" Sal cried. "We were born this way. We are this way. And like Rail I hope to die the same way you son of a bitch!"

"I hope that gives you some comfort." Michaels said not putting any real substances in what Sal said. "Now, we need to make a good cover story for when the others return from the wild goose chase. Tell them why there was no Drac-cul where I sent them."

"That why I'm here?" scoffed Sal. "You're a kidnapper, a blackmailer, and a murderer... and you're worried about losing face to the Quinns?"

"My position is very high. I can't afford to lose faith among the men."

"How much faith do you think they'll have if I transform right in front of them all?" she asked, going into werewolf mode.

"That would not be a good idea." he said. "You'll be killed... then so would Paul and Kenneth because they share the same blood."

"But they're human." she said, turning back to human. "You know that."

That's my personal view, yes. But I doubt the others would see it the same way. At the very least your brother willing collaborating with an abomination would not go well for him."

"Collaborating?" she asked, hearing the most ridiculous thing. "He's my brother."

"That may give him a little leeway but are you willing to put his life on that?" asked Michaels

Sal sank into the chair across from Michaels' desk saying nothing.

"Good. I'm glad you see things the right way." he said "First, I think we need to tell them the Drac-cul site was…"

Sal wasn't listening to him. All she could think was that she was putting the ones she loved in danger. Rail was dead. the vampire who tried to help was going to burn when the sun came up, and her brother could be killed just because she was his sister. A week ago, Sal had a plan to stop all this but didn't want to even think about it unless it was absolutely necessary. With everything that was happening… it became very necessary.

"It has to stop." she said

"Pardon?" Michaels asked, still focus on the cover story.

"It's going to stop. It's going to stop now." she said, pulling out the gun.

Michaels automatically raised his hands but didn't seem to be very worried.

"If we're going to do the 'killing me' thing aga---"

"I'm not gonna kill you." she said, cutting him off. "I'm gonna kill myself."

"What?" he said, with an obvious expression.

"The way I see it… it solves everything." she said. "I die. You lose your source. Paul and Kenny are safe."

"You won't do it"

"Why not?"

"Because you have no idea what could happen to them afterwards." he said, as a means of a threat.

"You won't do anything."

"Are you so sure?"

"Well just like you, Father. I have to have faith."

She turned the gun to her heart and started to squeeze the trigger.

"Tell my brother... I love him very much." she said.

"Michaels seeing the hammer of the gun cocking back rushed out of his chair to stop Sal but was stopped dead by the explosion... outside.

A little time before that Rail went sniffing for Danion. It took a few moments but she got the House Vampire scent and followed it. She avoided the Quinns through shadows and alleys and ran smack dab into Danion.

"You escaped." she cried

"You're alive." he said, with a stunned face. "They said you were shot. How---?"

Rail lifted her shirt to show the bulletproof vest. He was about to ask how she got it but then the answer was so obvious.

"Sage" he said.

They both laughed and the instinctively hugged each other. They broke apart (after a while) realizing what they were doing.

"Uhh... they knew we were here." Rail quickly said, to change the subject.

I know... the powerhouse was booby-trapped and..."

Danion caught something behind Rail. A small red light. He got a closer look and it and all came together on how everything went wrong.

"What is it?" asked Rail.

"Motion detector." he said, feeling like an idiot. "If these are all over town..."

"Then that's how they knew we were here." Rail said. "If that's working now..."

"We're outta here." said Danion.

They started to head out the alley when Rail got a whiff of something.

"Gasoline." she said.

Before Danion could say, 'What?'. A wave of flames flashed in front of them. They fell back in the alley checking to see if either one of them were singed.

Silver bullets won't kill a vampire. Wooden stakes won't kill werewolves. But fire...it does the job on both just fine.

The Quinn with the flame-thrower quickly advanced his position to get Rail and Danion. They were going to head out the other side but heard more Quinns coming that way. What those Quinns had for weapons the two didn't want to guess. So, with his arm around Rail, Danion flew them over the building to another alley.

"Find Sal, get her family, and get the hell out of here!" yelled Danion.

"What about you?" she asked.

"I'm going to lead the Quinns away." he said. "You see an opening. Take it and run."

"But what about you?" she repeated.

"Don't worry about me and go. GO!"

Rail was hesitant to leave but did to find Sal.

Danion came out of the alley so he could be a target for the Quinns. Six Quinns came up to confront him. Armed to the teeth with silver bullets and crossbows with the one with the flame-thrower wanted Danion for himself.

"I'll deal with this." the Quinn said. "Get the wolf."

The other Quinns left to go after Rail leaving the Quinn with the flame-thrower alone with Danion.

"Remember me?" Clipboard asked.

"Sorry... all you Quinns look alike to me." said Danion.

Truth be told Danion did remember the Quinn and knew that Clipboard was eager to settle the score for the warehouse.

"You took over my mind. Made me betray my friends... and my faith. You're going to pay for that." said Clipboard.

"Hate to tell you this but the way you fell... your faith was already in question.

I've always said, 'Never piss off anyone with a flame-thrower.' It's just common sense. Danion? He had other ideas because Clipboard started to chase him with that flame-thrower full-blast. He flew at a low height to make sure he didn't lose the Quinn. Danion insulted him with anything and everything he could to keep him angry enough not to notice where Danion was leading him... which was right back to the powerhouse of Brotherhood. Unfortunately, he was so busy with the Quinn behind him he didn't see the Quinns in front of him.

The bullet hit him in the shoulder knocking him out of the air. Like I said before silver bullets don't kill vampires but they sting like a bitch. Danion looked and saw that there were more Quinns at the powerhouse than before. He closed his eyes in disbelief over his fricking bad luck. Clipboard finally caught up with Danion on the ground. He saw the other Quinns by the powerhouse and it dawned on Clipboard. In a blind rage he could have easily burned down the powerhouse without realizing it.

"So that was you plan." he said to Danion.

"Basically."

"It's over abomination."

Clipboard stepped back and aimed very carefully. Danion didn't close his eyes or turn away. He was going to face his death but all along hoping that the werewolf got out with her friend and her family. As he felt the heat of the 'thrower' warming on his face ready to spit fire. He saw a light of hope behind Clipboard's back.

"Hmm... hot flame to burn the skin. I'm more of a leather strap girl myself but I'm flexible. At least that what I tell the girls." said Zarafinn.

Clipboard turned around to see who was speaking and was blinded by a bright flash of light. His eyes quickly teared up from the pain of that flash which made him accidentally fire the flame-thrower wildly into the other Quinns... and the powerhouse.

The building caught fire as well as a few Quinns. Danion got to his feet and looked at Zarafinn wondering what she was doing there. She looked back and gave him that smile that fairies are famous for having.

"I get back down if I were you." she said.

Danion looked at her not even question it and immediately hit the dirt. Two seconds later there was an explosion but it wasn't the powerhouse. It was a building across town. Then another building blew up down the street. The third explosion was the powerhouse. Other than the light coming from the building fires Brotherhood was completely in the dark.

Michaels looked out the window just in time to see the second explosion. When the third came and the lights went out Michaels knew Sal was involved.

"What have you done?!" he cried.

"I didn't do this" she said

"You expect me to believe that?" he yelled. "You lied about the Drac-cul and you're obviously lying now!"

Suddenly both their heads turned to the sounds of fighting and gunshots on the other side of the office door. Then in an instant a Quinn came flying through that door. When he landed on the floor, they could both clearly see he's throat was ripped out. Sal and Michaels then looked at the doorway and were both shocked to see Rail in full werewolf mode.

"We got to get out of here now!" she growled.

Snapping out of the shocked of seeing Rail one thing came to Sal.

"Paul. Kenny." she said. "Follow me."

Sal led Rail away completely forgetting about Michaels and the gun she unknowing let drop to the floor when she saw Rail was still alive. Leaving Michaels to pick that gun up and then pull out one of his own.

"You're right, Sal" he said, looking at the destruction outside. "This does need to end."

The Quinn that was guarding Paul and Kenny was quickly out of the way. Sal then rushed into the room to get her family out of Brotherhood.

"What the hell is going on?" Paul asked.

"I don't know but we're outta here." said Sal.

Sal looked at Kenny who was watching the excitement out the window.

"Where gonna have to fight our way out of here." she told her brother showing him yellow werewolf eyes.

Paul knew that meant a lot of blood would be flying and neither wanted Kenny to see it.

"Hey buddy... we gotta go." Paul told Kenny. "Now, I'm going to wrap you all the way up in this blanket. And I don't want you peeking out of it for any reason till I say, 'it's okay'"

"Okay, dad." Kenny smiled.

With Kenny wrapped up in Paul's arms Sal and Rail cleared a path of escape. Fires started spreading across Brotherhood as they heard two more explosions in the background. They were on their way out the building when they were stopped by a bullet passing them and hitting the wall. They looked back and saw Michaels pointing a gun at them. More precisely... at Sal. Rail started to move forward to face him but was held back by Sal.

"Get them out of here." she told Rail.

"No, I got a bulle---"

"Go... now." said Sal.

Rail rushed Paul and Kenny out the door while Sal faced Michaels. He shot at her and missed. Sal dodged each pull of the trigger until they both heard the click of the hammer. Sal double checked to see if he really was out of bullets. When she knew she charged at Michaels which was exactly what he had planned. He wanted Sal to charge him so he could pull out the gun she had for a clear shot. He aimed, prayed to God, and pulled the trigger for a very loud...click.

Did I forget to mention that was my gun Sal had?

I don't know how she found it but she must have realized it was the one that I threaten Rail with and assumed it was loaded with silver bullets. Luckily for Sal her assumption was wrong

Not so much for Father Michaels as Sal pinned him to the floor with a claw on his face.

"Why?" she asked? "Why all this? Why any of it?"

"Because it's the will of God." he said, with a firm conviction. "And you and the rest of the abominations are a curse upon his earth!"

"And he condones you kidnapping and threatening two innocents?"

"Hard decisions need to be made at times." he said. "And I pray for his greater glory that I and all like me will have the strength to do what is necessary... no matter what the cost."

"So-do-I." said Sal.

Outside Rail and Paul found a Quinn truck that luckily had the keys in it and drove out in front of the building where Sal was. Rail got out and started to head inside when Danion yelled out to her.

"What are you still doing here?!" he asked her.

"Sal's still inside. What the hell is happening?"

"The Consortia."

"They're after Sal."

"Right now, they're more interested in leveling this town." he said. "But you still need to get her out of here and not just outta this town or Denver. I mean Colorado... and I mean now!"

"Okay, I'll go... get her."

Sal walked out of the building in her human form with her hands, clothes, and mouth covered in blood. It was clear what happen but Rail still had to ask.

"Michaels? He's...?"

"Not going to bother us anymore." Sal answered.

"The two didn't question Sal's statement and Rail helped her in the truck but noticed Danion wasn't moving to join them.

"Come on, let's go." she told him.

"No... I'm going to stay and stall the Consortia while you go and get them out of here." Danion said. "Good luck. She'll need it. And if I don't see you again... it's been a whirl."

Rail got into the truck and it spun off out of Brotherhood. She watched as Danion got smaller in the distance wondering what was going to happen between him and the Consortia.

What was he going to do to stall them?

Would it work?

And most importantly... even though she wasn't admitting it (openly). Would she ever see Danion again?

5

Within thirty minutes Brotherhood was engulf in flames. Danion watched the burning from back on the cliff where he and Rail were earlier. Only this time the Lore with him was Zarafinn and Walsh.

"How did you set those charges?" he said.

They didn't answer. Walsh just smiled and Zarafinn giggled.

"Couldn't let me in on it?" Danion asked.

"Why? You made it out all right." said Zarafinn.

"True enough." said Walsh. "Now, about the traitor. Where is she?"

"She? How did you know---Ohh, forget it." Danion said. "So, were you ever going to tell me you knew it was Lore?"

"It was a possibility. We were more hoping that it was a human with a close association with Lore but we weren't sure until yesterday." said Walsh

"Yesterday? I just found out a few hours ago." said Danion.

Zarafinn and Walsh looked at each other.

"Yes, you did." Walsh said. "Now, where's the werewolf?"

"I don't know." Danion said.

The two looked at Danion with the obvious expression.

"I don't." he insisted to them. "Besides, doesn't it matter that she was being blackmail? Something I'm sure you already knew."

"Yes. To protect her brother and nephew." said Walsh.

"Her human brother and nephew." said Zarafinn.

"Forgive Zarafinn... she a bit of a separatist." Walsh said. "So, you don't know where the werewolf is or going?"

"No." Danion stressed.

"I hope that's the truth and not some kind of lover's loyalty" said Walsh.

"Pardon?" Danion asked, confused by that statement.

"Never mind." said Walsh.

"Hey, I done what you've asked me to do." said Danion. "Find the snitch and 'deal with it'. Well I found her. What she did was wrong. She knows that but she wanted to save family. You can't fault her for that. By the way the Quinn that was blackmailing her, Father Michaels. The one who's been a pain in the ass for two months is dead. Killed by her own claws no less. So, that should make you very happy. And she knows the Consortia's after her. Really don't think she's going to be sticking her head out in the community any time soon. So... it's over. Done. 'Dealt with'."

"Perhaps." Walsh said. "But this is about one of our own betraying us. With the werewolf we will show the Lore that this will not be tolerated under any circumstances. Michaels may not be a problem anymore but it will be just a matter of time before there's another like him. And will the next Lore do the same thing for whatever reason. Our best defense against the Quinns is the knowledge that we won't turn on each other. Because if we do we might as well line up and let them pick us off one by one."

Danion didn't say a word because he couldn't disagree even though he knew the special circumstances around it.

"Speaking of the Quinns, Michaels did make a point. You are the Lore's protectors. The Quinns are our biggest threat. So, why haven't you attacked them directly?" asked Danion.

"One, the Quinns don't think the Consortia exist. We prefer it that way. "said Walsh. "Two, the Quinns are not our greatest threat. And three... didn't we just do that?"

With that and a smile Walsh and Zarafinn flew off leaving Danion perplexed. Then he remembered that's the way it was last time.

"Two down, one to go. Then you're free from '91." Walsh cried down to him. "See you when you see us."

"Yeah... let's hope that's not any time soon." Danion said.

"He's not ready." Zarafinn told Walsh.

"I know." he said. "But I was right about him, though. He found the informant and sooner than *you* thought."

"He also let the girl go, you know?"

"Yes, but he also provided us with a tremendous opportunity against the Quinns. Give it a decade. He'll be ready to join us then."

"And the werewolf? We can't just let her go."

"Don't worry... finding her will be easy enough."

"And then what? 'Deal with her?'" she asked.

"What happens happens." said Walsh. "But perhaps being lenient on her can work out as well as it did with Danion. I mean, you have to admire the way she 'dealt' with Michaels."

By the time the other Quinns got back from their wild Drac-cul chase Brotherhood was beyond saving. They save what and whom they could and moved to a new location. The loss of the town, equipment, and lives were a huge blow to morale. Especially for the Quinn Squad Leader. He shook his head and prayed for an hour outside a locked door. A priest came out from that locked door and nodded his head in saying, 'It's done'.

 The SL walked inside and chained to a table was Father Michaels. His body was covered with claw marks and blood with his throat chewed out. He couldn't speak but he was still alive.

"Father Michaels. The wounds you have are healing now. In fact, they say you'll be up and around by day after tomorrow. As for your family... We don't know where they are and have to assume the worst."

Michaels looked at his body and realized that he should be dead. And from the damage knew that there was no natural way he could be 'up and around' in two days.

"You've been bitten, Father." the SL said. "Not once... but several times. We have given you last rites and we'll cremate the body just to make sure. I am sorry."

Michaels' eyes. His yellow werewolf eyes widened as he saw the SL aimed the gun barrel at his chest.

"May God have mercy on your immortal soul." he said, motioning a cross in front of his chest then firing three silver bullets into Michaels' heart.

Two days came and went and Paul had finished packing the truck they took from the Quinns so he, Kenny and Sal could leave

Denver. Once again, 'needless to say'... it was emotion departure for Sal and Rail.

"So, where are you headed?" Rail asked. "No... it's probably better I don't know."

"Wouldn't have to tell you if came with us." Sal offered. "But you don't need a life on the run."

"You be careful out there."

"I will. I can... thanks to you and your vampire."

"For the last...."

Rail was close to tears realizing that this was going to be the last time she would do anything with Sal again.

"He's not my vampire." finished Rail.

"You so want him."

"He's a vampire."

"Yeah... but you still want him, though." Sal said.

Sal got into truck and handed out a gift-wrapped package to Rail.

"Here." Sal said. "Something to say, 'Thank-you' with."

"What is it?"

"Open it and find out."

Paul turned the key to the truck. Rail and Sal gave each other the 'So... this is Good-bye' look when they heard the sound of the engine.

"No crying now." Sal said, herself close to tears.

"No crying." Rail said, taking Sal's hand to say, 'Good-bye'.

The truck slowly pulled away while they were still holding hands. Their arms stretched out until they finally had to let go. With a wave Rail saw Sal turn to look at her one last time as the truck turned to the corner and disappeared.

Rail closed her eyes and took a deep breath. 'It's over' she told herself. Sal and her family were gone and safe... and always hopefully one step ahead of the Consortia. She opened the gift Sal gave her and found a bottle of body spray.

"Oh, come on." laughed Rail.

Obviously, it was a gag gift she thought. It was probably going to make her stink worse than Sal did. Then she saw the note:

Just in case you

wanted to smell

nice for somebody.

Thank you forever.

Sal.

She sprayed the spray into the air and took a good whiff. It didn't reek. In fact, it smelled really nice. The aroma made her mind flash on romantic images which she enjoyed until she realized who the male lead was in those images.

"What the hell am I doing?"

"Open up." Rail said, knocking on Danion's door. "I can smell you in there."

Danion open the door stunned to see that Rail knew where he lived.

"How did you---"

"Sage." she said, walking inside.

I also asked her to tell him not to bother coming over to kill me, because I was moving. Too many people knew where I lived, damn it.

"Straight to the point." she told him. "This... thing that's been happening between us. It's not happening. Thanks for helping with Sal. I mean that but you and me... no. That's it. We shouldn't see each other anymore."

"I agree." he said.

"You do?"

"Yes... you're absolutely right. We should completely avoid one another."

She didn't know why she was disappointed. Rail knew it was better for both of them to stay away from each other. No matter how either one of them may have felt or maybe didn't feel but it was still disappointing.

"Okay then." she said. "Thanks again. It's been a... whirl. If I can pay you back for Sal, I will. Good-bye."

"So... Sal's gone?"

"Yeah." Rail said, in a sadden tone. "You think they'll find her?"

He knew that Rail wanted some encouragement that the Consortia wouldn't catch Sal. So, he reached out his hand to put on her shoulder but pulled it away at the last second.

"Let's hope not." he said, picking up the TV remote. "You were leaving, right?"

"Right."

She started to head out as Danion pressed the 'mute' bottom on the remote. Rail stopped when she heard the TV yell a familiar catch phrase and the roar of a huge crowd. She turned to see Danion plopped on the couch watching the WWF.

"Wrestling?" she snickered with surprised.

"Don't make fun. We all have our vices. This is mine." he said.

"Who's fighting?"

"See for yourself."

"Ohh, good match." she said immediately plopping herself next to Danion.

"Staying a while?" Danion asked.

"You mind?"

"Nah," he didn't mind suddenly catching something in the air. "'Sniff-Sniff.' What's that smell?"

"Oh, that's... something Sal sprayed on me. Last little joke." she lied. "Sorry."

"Don't be... it's nice. Like 'sniff' roses after it rains. I like it." he said.

Rail slightly turned her head towards Danion in response to his compliment.

"Okay." she smiled.

And so it began.

The story of how two ancient enemies... a werewolf and a vampire fell in love.

(and along the way eventually learned each other's names.)

Now comes the part where I say, 'And they lived happily ever...'

No.

Not quite yet.

You see old hates die hard. And those who hate will do anything unfortunately to keep the hate alive.

Confused? Don't be.

You'll understand soon enough.

Afterwords

Hi. If you're reading this it means that you've read and hopefully finished (with a little bit of enjoyment) the story that was laid upon you. And how did this story get started? Well, like most stories where the author 's a male it involves a girl.

Said girl was already taken and in love and I wasn't going to make any moves. I don't even really remember how the conversation of writing came about but she convinced me to write a little something and a week later the first chapter (and what I honestly thought would be the last) of C&SB was written. She liked the first chapter and encouraged me to write more. I did because I really enjoyed getting some praise and at that time of my life I really wasn't getting a lot of it... mostly because I wasn't doing a lot to get praise.

As I wrote more I started to head to the local book stores. Partly to get some inspiration but mostly to imagine my name among the sea of published authors. There I met and made friends with the staff (mostly girls) and one subjected I put my story on the net.

I was hesitant mostly because I'm a cyber-moron who didn't know how to download (...or upload) a story on a website but after more than a few tries I got Danion and Rail out there on the World Wide Web. Got some nice reviews and encouragement to write more then something happened. I found out that a movie was coming out that had the same basic premise as the story I had writing.

Well, you know what I was thinking anyone who read this story after that movie comes out would just think I copied the idea.

So, what would be the point of finishing the story? But after a depressing period of moping I finally lighted a fire under my ass and started writing again. Yeah, this movie was going to overshadow my story but at the very least people were going to know that I wasn't a plagiarist.

I finished the third (and probably final) act of Danion and Rail and then sadly had to do what most people had to do... start living in the real world. I got a job (a temp job), paid my bills, and the next thing I knew ten years rolled by in my life. The job was good. The people were good and for a temp job it paid more than most permanents one, so I kept working but I stopped writing. My life became a routine of waking up, going to work, keeping the lights on, and going back to sleep. I wanted to write and I did... in my head but when it came to putting things on paper the desire was there but not the drive which put me on an off and on depression.

But also in that period the internet made a quantum leap in the literary world through the digital world becoming the best friend to would-be-writers everywhere. Anyone with an idea, a computer, and the stones could bypass a disapproving publisher who couldn't or wouldn't understand their work by going directing to the masses for instant approval... or disapproval. It was all depending if they liked what they read.

I decided to get the stones and with a lot of encouragement from family members started the process of making an E-book and in turn something kind of awesome happened... the drive to write came back again. I had a new idea and started writing. During work I wrote on scratch paper and cleaned it up in a notebook at home

Then one day I came home and found out I was fired from my job... and I was pretty okay with it. For nearly ten years I was a temp. I didn't want it to be twenty years and say the same thing.

I wanted to say I did a little bit more with my life and as the old song goes, '**DON'T DREAM IT. BE IT**'!

So, I focused on updating Danion and Rail while finding a new job (because I still needed to keep the lights on) I also found a very talent and extremely patient artist who could bring C&SB visually to life. All three got accomplice and the final results is what you just read.

But through it all I still always worried that people would say, 'He just stole the idea from that movie'. Then it just hit me. Didn't this other writer get the basic premise from a play that was written a long ago? And since that play's opening hasn't countless books, movies, TV shows, and songs been based on the same theme? I wasn't a plagiarist. I just was a guy who came up with the same idea around same time. It does happen. It's just that the other writer got his story turned into a movie and today the big screen tends to trump the written word.

But in the end... I just had to say, 'Screw it!'

It's one of the reasons you're reading afterwords instead of forewords. I want you to make your own opinion about Danion and Rail and not be impress by pretty words about an unknown author before the story. The story should impress you first or not impress you. I'll find out either way making my decision to continue with ACTII a lot easier but bottom-line... I did it. I got the stones to roll the dices. What they'll come up as... Who knows?

Frank Webb.

Made in the USA
Columbia, SC
14 December 2024